Pelagie Doane

# THE YELLOW PHANTOM

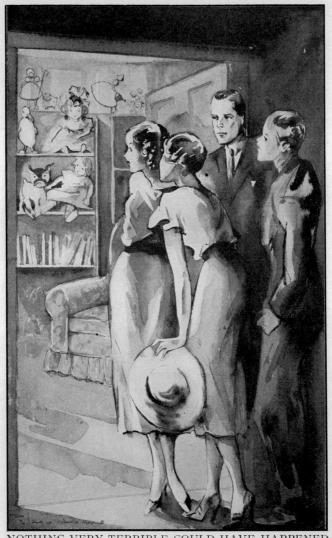

NOTHING VERY TERRIBLE COULD HAVE HAPPENED
IN THIS ROOM.

A JUDY BOLTON MYSTERY

# THE YELLOW PHANTOM

BY

MARGARET SUTTON

AUTHOR OF
THE INVISIBLE CHIMES
THE GHOST PARADE, ETC.

*ILLUSTRATED BY*

PELAGIE DOANE

GROSSET & DUNLAP
PUBLISHERS    NEW YORK

*To My Mother and Father*

# CONTENTS

# CONTENTS

## viii CONTENTS

# THE YELLOW PHANTOM

## CHAPTER I

### A MYSTERIOUS TELEGRAM

"Goodbye, Judy! Goodbye, Irene! Don't like New York so well that you won't want to come home!"

"Don't keep them too long, Pauline! Farringdon will be as dead as so many bricks without them. Even the cats will miss Blackberry. Make him wave his paw, Judy!"

"Don't forget to write!"

"Goodbye, Pauline! Goodbye, Judy! Goodbye, Irene!"

"Goodbye! Goodbye!"

And Peter's car was off, bearing the last load of campers back to their home town.

Judy Bolton watched them out of sight. They were taking the familiar road, but she and

1

Irene Lang would soon be traveling in the other direction. Pauline Faulkner had invited them for a visit, including Judy's cat in the invitation, and they were going back with her to New York.

A long blue bus hove into view, and all three girls hailed it, at first expectantly, then frantically when they saw it was not stopping. It slowed down a few feet ahead of them, but when they attempted to board it the driver eyed Blackberry with disapproval.

"Can't take the cat unless he's in a crate."

"He's good," Judy began. "He won't be any trouble——"

"Can't help it. Company's rules." And he was about to close the door when Judy's quick idea saved the situation.

"All right, he's *in a crate*," she declared with vigor as she thrust the cat inside her own pretty hatbox. The hats she hastily removed and bundled under one arm.

The driver had to give in. He even grinned a bit sheepishly as the girls took their seats, Pauline and Irene together, "Because," Judy insisted as she took the seat just behind them, "I have Blackberry."

The other passengers on the bus were regarding the newcomers with amused interest. A ten-year-old boy brought forth a ball of twine and rolled it playfully in Blackberry's direction. An old lady made purring noises through her lips. Everyone seemed to be nodding and smiling. Everyone except the serious young man across the aisle. He never turned his head.

Judy nudged the two friends in the seat ahead of her and confided a desire to do something—anything to make him look up.

"Why, Judy," Irene replied, shocked. "I've been watching that man myself and he's —he's——"

"Well, what?"

"Almost my ideal."

"Silly!" Judy laughed. "I'd like to bet he wouldn't be so ideal if I did something to disturb those precious papers that he's reading."

"I dare you!" Pauline said.

Sixteen or not, the dare tempted Judy. It was an easy matter to let Blackberry out of the hatbox in her arms and down into the aisle. The cat's plumelike tail did the rest.

The man looked up. But, to Judy's surprise,

he looked up with a smile. Irene, all contrition, hastened to apologize.

"No harm done," he returned good-naturedly and began collecting his scattered papers. Soon he had them rearranged and resumed his reading. There were a great many typewritten sheets of paper, and he seemed to be reading critically, scratching out something here and adding something there.

"You were wrong," Irene said, turning to Judy. "See how nice he was."

"I should have known better than to dare a girl like you," Pauline put in.

"It was horrid of me," Judy admitted, now almost as interested as Irene in the strange young man. Not because he was Judy's ideal —a man who wouldn't notice a cat until its tail bumped into him—but because the papers on his lap might be important. And she had disturbed them.

The man, apparently unaware that the accident had been anybody's fault, continued reading and correcting. Judy watched her cat carefully until the stack of papers was safely inside his portfolio again.

"That's finished," he announced as though

speaking to himself. He screwed the top on his fountain pen, placed it in his pocket and then turned to the girls. "Nice scenery, wasn't it?"

"It was," Judy replied, laughing, "but you didn't seem to be paying much attention to it."

"I've been over this road a great many times," he explained, "and one does tire of scenery, like anything else. Passengers in the bus are different."

"You mean different from scenery?"

"Yes, and from each other. For instance, you with your ridiculous cat and your golden-haired friend who apologized for you and that small, dark girl are three distinct types."

Judy regarded him curiously. She had never thought of herself or either of the other girls as "types." Now she tried to analyze his meaning.

Their lives had certainly been different. Judy and Pauline, although of independent natures, had always felt the security of dependence upon their parents while Irene's crippled father depended solely upon her. This responsibility made her seem older than her years— older and younger, too. She never could acquire Pauline's poise or Judy's fearlessness.

In appearance, too, they were different. Her first vacation had done wonders for Irene Lang. Now her usually pale cheeks glowed with healthy color, and her eyes were a deeper, happier blue. Two weeks of sunshine had tanned her skin and brought out all the gold in her hair.

Pauline, too, had acquired a becoming tan which made her hair look darker than ever and contrasted strangely with her keen, light blue eyes.

The sun had not been quite so kind to Judy. It had discovered a few faint freckles on her nose and given her hair a decided reddish cast. But Judy didn't mind. Camp life had been exciting—boating, swimming and, as a climax, a thrilling ride in Arthur Farringdon-Pett's new airplane.

The young man beside Judy was a little like Arthur in appearance—tall, good-looking but altogether too grown-up and serious. Judy liked boys to make jokes now and then, even tease the way her brother, Horace, did. Peter teased her, too.

"Queer," she thought, "to miss being teased."

This stranger seemed to like serious-minded people and presently changed the conversation to books and music, always favorite topics with Irene. Then Judy spoke about the work that he was doing but learned nothing except that "finished" in his case meant that he had succeeded in putting his papers back in their original sequence.

"And if you girls were all of the same type," he added, "I doubt if I would have forgiven you your prank."

"I guess he doesn't care for my type," Judy whispered to the other two girls a little later.

"Mine either," Pauline returned with a laugh. "At least he wouldn't if he knew I dared you."

"Do you suppose," Irene asked naïvely, "that he cares for my type?"

She looked very pathetic as she said that, and Judy, remembering Irene's misfortunes, slid into the seat beside her and put a loving arm about her shoulder.

"I care for your type," she said. "So why worry about what a stranger thinks?"

"I'm not," Irene said, belying her answer with a wistful look in the stranger's direction.

He was still absorbed in the mountain of typewritten pages that he held on his knee. It
seemed that his work, whatever it was, en-
grossed him completely. He was again making
corrections and additions with his pen. Judy
noticed a yellow slip of paper on the seat beside him and called the other girls' attention
to it.

"It looks like a telegram," she whispered,
"and he keeps referring to it."

"Telegrams are usually bad news," Irene replied.

The young man sat a little distance away
from them and, to all appearances, had forgotten their existence. Girl-like, they discussed
him, imagining him as everything from a poli-
tician to a cub reporter, finally deciding that,
since he lived in Greenwich Village, he must be
an artist. Irene said she liked to think of him
as talented. A dreamer, she would have called
him, if it had not been for his practical interest
in the business at hand—those papers and that
telegram.

It was dark by the time they reached New
York. The passengers were restless and eager
to be out of the bus. The young man hastily

crammed his typewritten work into his portfolio and Judy noticed, just as the bus stopped, that he had forgotten the telegram. She and Irene both made a dive for it with the unfortunate result that when they stood up again each of them held a torn half of the yellow slip.

"Just our luck!" exclaimed Irene. "Now we can't return it to him. Anyway, he's gone."

"We could piece it together," Pauline suggested, promptly suiting her actions to her words. When the two jagged edges were fitted against each other, this is what the astonished girls read:

DALE MEREDITH
PLEASANT VALLEY PA
CUT ART SHOP ROBBERY STOP FIFTY THOUSAND
IS PLENTY STOP ONE MAN MURDERED INTERESTS
RANDALL STOP DISCUSS TERMS MONDAY
EMILY GRIMSHAW

Irene was the first to finish reading.

"Good heavens! What would *he* know about robbery and murder?" she exclaimed, staring first at the telegram in Pauline's hand and then at the empty seat across the aisle.

"Why, nothing that I can think of. He didn't seem like a crook. The telegram may be in code," Pauline mused as she handed the torn pieces to Judy. "I like his name—Dale Meredith."

"So do I. But Emily Grimshaw——"

"All out! Last stop!" the bus driver was calling. "Take care of that cat," he said with a chuckle as he helped the girls with their suitcases.

They were still wondering about the strange telegram as they made their way through the crowd on Thirty-fourth Street.

# CHAPTER II

## IRENE'S DISCOVERY

A TAXI soon brought the girls to the door of Dr. Faulkner's nineteenth century stone house. The stoop had been torn down and replaced by a modern entrance hall, but the high ceilings and winding stairways were as impressive as ever.

Drinking in the fascination of it, Judy and Irene followed the man, Oliver, who carried their bags right up to the third floor where Pauline had a sitting room and a smaller bedroom all to herself. The former was furnished with a desk, sofa, easy chairs, numerous shaded lamps, a piano and a radio.

Here the man left them with a curt, " 'Ere you are.''

"And it's good to have you, my dears,'' the more sociable housekeeper welcomed them. Soon she was bustling around the room setting their bags in order. She offered to help unpack.

11

"Never mind that now, Mary," Pauline told her. "We're dead tired and I can lend them some of my things for tonight."

"Then I'll fix up the double bed in the next room for your guests and leave you to yourselves," the kind old lady said.

As soon as she had closed the door Judy lifted her cat out of the hatbox. With a grateful noise, halfway between a purr and a yowl, Blackberry leaped to the floor and began, at once, to explore the rooms.

"His padded feet were made for soft carpets," Judy said fondly.

"How do you suppose he'd like gravel?" Pauline asked.

"Oh, he'd love it!" Judy exclaimed. "You know our cellar floor is covered with gravel, and he sleeps down there."

"Is this gravel in the cellar?" Irene asked, beginning to get an attack of shivers.

Pauline laughed. "Goodness, no! It's on the roof garden." She walked across the room and flung open a door. "Nothing shivery about that, is there?"

"Nothing except the thought of standing on the top of one of those tall buildings," Irene said, gazing upward as she followed Pauline.

The view fascinated Judy. Looking out across lower New York, she found a new world of gray buildings and flickering lights. In the other direction the Empire State Building loomed like a sentinel.

"I never dreamed New York was like this," she breathed.

"It grows on a person," Pauline declared. "I would never want to live in any other city. No matter how bored or how annoyed I may be during the day, at night I can always come up here and feel the thrill of having all this for a home."

"I wish I had a home I could feel that way about," Irene sighed.

The garden was too alluring for the girls to want to leave it. Even Blackberry had settled himself in a bed of geraniums. These and other plants in enormous boxes bordered the complete inclosure. Inside were wicker chairs, a table and a hammock hung between two posts.

"This is where I do all my studying," Pauline said, "and you two girls may come up here and read if you like while I'm at school."

"At school?" Judy repeated, dazed until she

thought of something that she should have considered before accepting Pauline's invitation. Of course Pauline would be in school. She hadn't been given a holiday as the girls in Farringdon had when their school burned down. Judy and Irene would be left to entertain themselves all day unless Dr. Faulkner had some plans for them. Judy wondered where he was.

After they had gone inside again, that is, all of them except Blackberry who seemed to have adopted the roof garden as a permanent home, she became curious enough to ask.

"Oh, didn't I tell you?" Pauline said in surprise. "Father is away. A medical conference in Europe. He's always going somewhere like that, but he'll be home in two or three weeks."

"Then we'll be alone for three weeks?" Irene asked, dismayed.

"Why not?" Pauline returned indifferently. "There's nothing to be afraid of with servants in the house."

But Irene was not used to servants. Ever since her father became disabled she had waited on herself and kept their shabby little house in apple-pie order. The house was closed now and their few good pieces of furniture put in stor

age. All summer long there would not be any
rent problems or any cooking. Then, when fall
came, she and her father would find a new
home. Where it would be or how they would
pay for it worried Irene when she thought
about it. She tried not to think because Dr.
Bolton had told her she needed a rest. Her
father, a patient of the doctor's, was under-
going treatments at the Farringdon Sanitarium. The treatments were being given
according to Dr. Bolton's directions but not by
him as Judy's home, too, was closed for the
summer. Her parents had not intended to stay
away more than a week or two, but influenza
had swept the town where they were visiting.
Naturally, the doctor stayed and his wife with
him. Judy's brother, a reporter and student
of journalism, had gone to live in the college
dormitory.

Thus it was that both girls knew they could
not return to Farringdon no matter how home-
sick they might be. They had the cat for comfort and they had each other. Ever since Irene
had come to work in Dr. Bolton's office these
two had been like sisters. Lois, Lorraine,
Betty, Marge, Pauline—all of them were

friends.  But Irene and Honey, the other girl
who had shared Judy's home, were closer than
that.  Judy felt with them.  She felt with Irene
the longing of the other girl for something to
hold fast to—a substantial home that could not
be taken away at every whim of the landlord,
just enough money so that she could afford to
look her best and the security of some strong
person to depend upon.

"Will your school last long?" Irene was asking the dark-haired girl.

"Not long enough," Pauline sighed, reveal-
ing the fact that she too had troubles.

"Then you'll be free?" Irene went on, un-
mindful of the sigh.  "We can go places together?  You'll have time to show us around."

Pauline shrugged her shoulders.  "Don't
talk about time to me.  Time will be my middle
name after I graduate.  There isn't a single
thing I really want to do, least of all stay at
home all day.  College is a bore unless you're
planning a career.  What do you intend to do
when you're through school?"

"I hadn't planned," Irene said, "except that
I want time to read and go ahead with my

music. Of course I'll keep house somewhere for Dad. It will be so nice to have him well again, and I love keeping house."

"What about your work for my father?" Judy asked.

Irene's eyes became troubled. "He doesn't really need me any more. I know now, Judy, that you just made that position for me. It was lovely of you, but I—I'd just as soon not go back where I'm not needed. Your father trusts too many people ever to get rich and he could use that money he's been paying me."

"Don't feel that way about it," Judy begged.

Irene's feelings, however, could not easily be changed, and with both girls having such grave worries the problem bid fair to be too great a one for even Judy to solve. Solving problems, she hoped, would eventually be her career for she planned to become a regular detective with a star under her coat. Now she confided this ambition to the other two girls.

"A detective!" Pauline gasped. "Why, Judy, only men are detectives. Can you imagine anyone taking a mere girl on the police force?"

"Chief Kelly, back home, would take her this very minute if she applied," Irene declared.

Pauline nodded, easily convinced. This practical, black-haired, blue-eyed girl had helped Judy solve two mysteries and knew that she had talent. But Pauline didn't want to meet crooks. She didn't want to be bothered with sick or feeble-minded people and often felt thankful that her father, a brain specialist, had his offices elsewhere. Pauline wanted to meet cultured people who were also interesting.

"People, like that man we met on the bus," she said, "who read and can discuss books intelligently. I'd hate to think of his being mixed up in anything crooked."

"You can't *make* me believe that he was," Irene put in with a vigor quite rare for her. "Couldn't you just see in his eyes that he was real?"

"I didn't look in his eyes," Judy returned with a laugh, "but you can be sure I'll never be satisfied until we find out what that mysterious telegram meant."

In the days that followed Judy learned that the mere mention of the stranger's name, Dale Meredith, would cause either girl to cease worrying about a home or about a career, as the case might be.

"It's almost magical," she said to herself and had to admit that the spell was also upon her. Perhaps a dozen times a day she would puzzle over the torn papers in her pocketbook. But then, it was Judy's nature to puzzle over things. It was for that reason that she usually chose detective stories whenever she sat down with a book. That hammock up there on the roof garden was an invitation to read, and soon Judy and Irene had finished all the suitable stories in Dr. Faulkner's library. They had seen a few shows, gazed at a great many tall buildings, and found New York, generally, less thrilling from the street than it had been from the roof garden.

Pauline sensed this and worried about entertaining her guests. "How would you like to go and see Grant's Tomb today?" she suggested.

"For Heaven's sake, think of something a little more exciting than that," Judy exclaimed thoughtlessly. "I'd rather find a library somewhere and then lie and read something in the hammock."

"So would I," agreed Irene, relieved that Judy hadn't wanted to see the tomb.

"Well, if a library's all you want," Pauline said, "why not walk along with me and I'll show you one on my way to school."

"A big one?" Judy asked.

"No, just a small one. In fact, it's only a bookshop with a circulating library for its customers."

Judy sighed. It would seem nice to see something small for a change. She never recognized this library at all until they were almost inside the door. Then her eyes shone.

What an interesting place it was! On the counters were quaint gifts and novelties as well as books. The salesladies all wore smocks, like artists, and had the courtesy to leave the girls alone. Pauline had to hurry on to school but left Judy and Irene to browse. Before long they had discovered a sign reading MYSTERY AND ADVENTURE. That was what Judy liked. Rows and rows of new books, like soldiers, marched along the shelves.

"What a lot of flying stories," Irene said, absently removing one of them from its place.

"And murder mysteries," Judy added. "It's always a temptation to read them. *Murders in Castle Stein . . .*"

She started back as her eye caught the author's name.

It was Dale Meredith!

# CHAPTER III

## A DARING SCHEME

THRILLED by her discovery, Judy removed the torn pieces of telegram from her purse and began unraveling the mystery, bit by bit. Irene looked on, trembling with excitement.

"'CUT ART SHOP ROBBERY STOP FIFTY THOUSAND IS PLENTY STOP . . .' *Art Shop Robbery!* That sounds like a title! And someone wanted him to cut it to fifty thousand words—just a nice length for a book. That must have been what he was doing on the bus, cutting down the number of words on those typewritten pages."

"Why, of course," Irene agreed. "I always knew you were gifted, Judy, but can you explain this?" She pointed.

"'ONE MAN MURDERED INTERESTS RANDALL . . .' Easy as pie! Another title and a publisher."

Judy tossed her head with a self-satisfied air of importance. Every one of their questions might be answered in the classified directory.

They found a telephone booth near by and a directory on the shelf beside it. Promptly turning to the list of publishing houses, Judy's finger traveled down one complete page and half of another, but no Randall could she find. With a sigh of disappointment she turned to look again at the telegram:

"DISCUSS TERMS MONDAY

"EMILY GRIMSHAW"

What sort of person was she? A relative? No. Relatives didn't discuss terms with authors. Wives and sweethearts didn't either. They might discuss his books, but not terms. Anyway Irene hoped that Dale Meredith had no wife or sweetheart, certainly not a sweetheart with a name like Emily Grimshaw. That name sounded as harsh to the ears as Dale Meredith sounded musical.

Flipping the pages of the directory, Judy came upon the answer to their question:

"AUTHOR'S AGENTS (*See* Literary Agents)."

"That might be it!"

She turned to the place and, beginning at the

top of the page, both girls searched eagerly through the G's.

"Greenspan, Grier, Grimshaw . . ."

The name was Emily and the address was a number on Madison Square. Irene was so excited that she declared she could feel her heart thumping under her slip-on sweater.

"I'd give anything to meet him again, Judy! Anything!"

And suddenly Judy wanted to meet him too, not for her own sake but for Irene's. A bold plan began to take shape in her mind. If she and Irene found positions in Emily Grimshaw's office Dale Meredith would never know that it had not been a simple coincidence. It would be such fun—this scheming. It would give them something to do and if Judy's plan worked it might even solve the problem of Pauline's career.

"Of course Emily Grimshaw may not hire us," Judy said after she had outlined the scheme and won Irene's approval. "But, at any rate, it's worth trying. We won't need to tell her it's only for a few weeks when Pauline will be there to step right into the position. I wonder how you get to Madison Square."

She stopped a policeman to ask him and found it to be within easy walking distance.

"We might as well go now," Irene agreed.

Perhaps if they thought about it too long they might lose heart and not attempt it.

The literary agent's office was located in an old hotel on the northeast side of the square. The building looked as if it had been unchanged for a century. In the lobby Judy and Irene paused, surveying the quaint furniture and mural decorations before they mustered enough courage to inquire at the desk for Emily Grimshaw.

"Who's calling?" the clerk asked tartly.

"Tell her——" Judy hesitated. "Tell her it's two girls to see her on business."

The message was relayed over the switchboard and presently the clerk turned and said, "She will see one of you. First stairway to the left. Fourth floor."

"Only one——" Judy began.

"She always sees one client at a time. The other girl can wait."

"That's right. I—I'll wait," Irene stammered.

"But you wanted the position——"

"I don't now. Suppose she asked about experience."

"You've had a little. You stand a better chance than I do."

"Not with your nerve, Judy," Irene said. "This place gives me the shivers. You're welcome to go exploring dark halls if you like. I'd rather sit here in the lobby and read Dale Meredith's book."

"Oh, so that's it? Make yourself comfortable," Judy advised with a laugh. "I may be gone a long, long time."

"Not if she finds out how old you are."

"Hush!" Judy reproved. "Don't I look dignified?"

She tilted her hat a little more to the left and dabbed a powder puff on her nose. The puff happened not to have any powder on it but it gave her a grown-up, courageous feeling. And she was to have a great need of courage in the hour that followed.

## CHAPTER IV

### HOW THE SCHEME WORKED

THE adventure lost some of its thrill with no one to share it. Judy hadn't an idea in the world how to find the fourth floor as she could see no stairway and no elevator.

Taking a chance, she opened one of several doors. It opened into a closet where cleaning supplies were kept. Judy glanced at the dusty floor and wondered if anybody ever used them.

This was fun! She tried another door and found it locked. But the third door opened into a long hall at the end of which was the stairway.

"A regular labyrinth, this place," she thought as she climbed. "I wonder if Emily Grimshaw will be as queer as her hotel."

There were old-fashioned knockers on all the doors, and Judy noticed that no two of them were alike. Emily Grimshaw had her name on the glass door of her suite, and the knocker

was in the shape of a witch hunched over a
steaming caldron. Judy lifted it and waited.

"Who's there?" called a mannish voice from
within.

"Judy Bolton. They told me at the desk
that you would see me."

"Come on in, then. Don't stand there bang-
ing the knocker."

"I beg your pardon," Judy said meekly as
she entered. "I didn't quite understand."

"It's all right. Who sent you?"

"Nobody. I came myself. I found your
name in the classified directory."

"Oh, I see. Another beginner."

Emily Grimshaw sat back in her swivel chair
and scrutinized Judy. She was a large woman
dressed in a severely plain brown cloth dress
with sensible brown shoes to match. Her iron-
gray hair was knotted at the back of her head.
In fact, the only mark of distinction about her
whole person was the pair of glasses perched
on the high bridge of her nose and the wide,
black ribbon suspended from them. Although
an old woman, her face was not wrinkled.
What few lines she had were deep furrows that
looked as if they belonged there. Judy could

imagine Emily Grimshaw as a middle-aged woman but never as a girl.

The room was, by no means, a typical office. If it had not been for the massive desk littered with papers and the swivel chair it would not have looked like an office at all. Three of the four walls were lined with bookshelves.

"Is this where you do all your work?" Judy asked.

"And why not? It's a good enough place."

"Of course," Judy explained herself quickly. "But I supposed you would have girls working for you. It must keep you busy doing all this yourself."

"Hmm! It does. I like to be busy."

Judy took a deep breath. How, she wondered, was she to put her proposition before this queer old woman without seeming impudent. It was the first time in her life she had ever offered her services to anyone except her father.

"You use a typewriter," she began.

"Look here, young woman," Emily Grimshaw turned on her suddenly, "if you're a writer, say so. And if you've come here looking for a position——"

"That's it exactly," Judy interrupted. "I'm sure I could be of some service to you."

"What?"

"I might typewrite letters for you."

"I do that myself. Haven't the patience to dictate them."

"Perhaps I could help you read and correct manuscripts," Judy suggested hopefully.

The agent seemed insulted. "Humph!" she grunted. "Much you know about manuscripts!"

"I may know more than you think," Judy came back at her. It was hard to be patient with this irritable old lady. Certainly she would never have chosen such an employer if it had not been for the possibility of meeting Dale Meredith again. Irene had taken such a fancy to him.

"Lucky she doesn't know that," thought Judy as she watched her fumbling through a stack of papers on her desk. Finally she produced a closely written page of note paper and handed it to the puzzled girl.

"If you know so much about manuscripts," she charged. "What would you do with a page like that?"

Half hoping that the handwriting was Dale Meredith's, Judy reached out an eager hand. The agent was watching her like a cat and, as she read, a hush settled over the room.  Emily Grimshaw was putting Judy to a test.

# CHAPTER V

THE paper that Judy held in her hand was a
jumble of morbid poetry written in what could
have been a beautiful hand.  Actually, it was
an almost unreadable scrawl.  In some places
the rhymes were in perfect sequence, but in
others the poet had wandered away from what
must have been the theme to play with words
that apparently amused her.  Finally Judy
made out this much:

> When Love turns thief, grief, sheaf, oh, dis-
> belief
> 'Tis memories that sting, ring, cling like any-
> thing.
> When Joy departs, starts, smarts, makes
> broken hearts . . .
> Too close I kept you, Joy.
> Should I have shared my toy?
> Tossed you to human tomcats to destroy?
> They say you're dead.  They lie!
> You cannot die!
> You drifted off in air
> To share

32

Your hair
Your fair white skin,
The very dress you wear.
IT'S MINE!  YOU'RE MINE!
I'll find you if I choke
In smoke . . .
My Joy my toy my Joy my toy my Joy JOY
    J O Y
My head's on fire!
'Tis memories that burn.
Better to crumble in a tower of flame
Than sit with ghosts awaiting your return.

How could anyone crumble in a tower of flame, Judy wondered.  Oh, well, she supposed it was just a lot of melancholy words jumbled together to give the reader the creeps.  Certainly she was not going to give Emily Grimshaw the satisfaction of knowing that it had impressed her.

"With the poet's permission," she looked up and said, "I would take out a few lines and then type the poem on a clean sheet of paper."

"I have the poet's permission," Emily Grimshaw replied shortly.  And, after a pause, "What lines would you take out?"

"Half of some of them and all of this one." Judy pointed.  "The words 'Joy' and 'toy' are repeated too many times."

"That's the first thing one notices," the old lady replied, evidently pleased with Judy's suggestion. "How do you like that poetry?"

"I *don't* like it," the girl replied frankly. "It sounds as if the writer had a distorted idea of life. It depresses a person just to read it."

"There are people who like to be depressed."

"I suppose so," Judy answered wearily. She could see that the conversation was getting them nowhere, and Irene must be dreadfully tired of waiting. Besides, she did not care to stand and argue with as queer a person as Emily Grimshaw seemed to be. Why, she was more peculiar, even, than the matron at camp or the queer old lady who ran the dog and cat hospital.

"Would you like me to sit down and type the poem for you now?" Judy suggested. "Then you could see exactly what I mean."

The old lady consented with a wave of her hand, and Judy set to work. The task was not an easy one, and when she had finished cutting out all the queer-sounding lines the poem was about half its original length. Hardly knowing whether to expect praise or criticism, she

handed the revised poem to Emily Grimshaw
and waited while she read:

When Love turns thief 'tis memories that
    sting;
When Joy departs 'tis memories that burn.
Better to crumble in a tower of flame
Than sit with ghosts awaiting your return.

"These are the four best lines," Judy pointed
out when she had finished reading. "I took out
parts of the first three lines and switched the
last three over toward the beginning. It's more
coherent that way if anyone should ever try to
figure it out. But the middle stanza must either
stay as it is or be taken out entirely. Which
do you think, Miss Grimshaw?"

"I'd take it out," she declared. "There's
too much truth in it."

Too much truth? A person who could not
die! Who drifted off in air! Judy would have
said exactly the opposite. It was too impossible.

"Didn't the poet explain what she meant
when the manuscript was delivered?" she
asked.

"Explain it! Humph! Jasper Crosby ex-

pects me to explain it. He's the poet's
brother," the agent pointed out. "He brings
me the stuff in just such a jumble as this."

The pile before her on the desk eloquently
illustrated the word "jumble." Old envelopes,
bills, sales sheets, anything that happened to be
about, had been used for the poet's snatches
of verse.

"It must take a lot of time to rearrange
them," Judy ventured.

"Time! That's just it. Time and patience,
too. But Jasper Crosby cares as much about
the value of my time as a newborn baby. He
never talks except in terms of dollars and cents.
'What can you make out of this?' 'How much
do we get out of that?' And expects me to re-
write half of it! It's trying my patience to the
limit, I can tell you. If I weren't so fond of the
poet I would have given it up years ago. Her
verses used to be of quite a different type. You
know *Golden Girl?*"

"You mean the popular song? Of course
I do."

"Well, she wrote that twenty years ago. It's
just recently been set to music."

Judy was becoming interested. As well as holding a promise of many new and charming acquaintances for herself and the other two girls the work was sure to be fascinating. Emily Grimshaw seemed pleased with the changes she had made in the poem, but it was best not to hurry her decision. Judy could see that she needed an assistant, but to make the agent see it also would require tact and patience.

In the course of another half hour Emily Grimshaw had made up her mind. Judy was to report at her office the following day. No mention had been made of Irene as Judy knew her chances of holding the position were slim enough without asking an additional favor. But she felt sure that her new employer would not object to the presence of both girls in the office after she had grown accustomed to the idea of being helped.

"And if she does object," Irene said cheerfully, "I'll apply for a position with Dale Meredith's publisher."

Eager to tell Pauline of their adventure, they walked toward the subway entrance and arrived just as the school girls were coming home.

"We found out who that man we met on the bus is," Judy announced the moment she saw Pauline. "He's an author and has written stacks and stacks of books. We bought one to read in our spare time."

"Really?"

"It's the honest truth," Irene declared. "I read ten chapters today while I was waiting for Judy. And what do you think? She has accepted a position in Emily Grimshaw's office."

Pauline stared. "The woman who sent that telegram? Who on earth is she and where did you find out?"

"In the classified telephone directory," Judy confessed. "She's Dale Meredith's literary agent, though why he should pick such a crotchety old woman to sell his stories is beyond me. I thought, at first, she was going to bite my head off. But she found out she couldn't frighten me so she decided to hire me. When she calms down a bit she'll probably let Irene help her, too."

"Imagine!" Irene exclaimed, still bubbling with enthusiasm, "our own spending money

and an opportunity to meet the most interesting people——''

''You mean Dale Meredith?''

Did Judy imagine it or was there the smallest
trace of bitterness in Pauline's voice?

''Well, perhaps I do,'' Irene replied.

# CHAPTER VI

## THE NEW YELLOW GOWN

IN SPITE of the opportunity presented, a whole week passed by without a sign of the handsome young author. Judy's suggestion that Irene might help in the office had been flatly ignored, but she was still hoping that Emily Grimshaw would change her mind. In the meantime Irene occupied herself with Dale Meredith's books and Pauline's piano.

Little by little Judy became accustomed to her employer's eccentricities, and meeting unusual people was an everyday occurrence. Jasper Crosby, of all the people she met, was the only one who seemed to resent her presence in the office. He came in, bringing an old shoe box stuffed with more poetry by the author of *Golden Girl*. The box was poked full of tiny holes. Judy's curiosity got the better of her and she asked the reason.

"So the verses can breathe, simpleton," he replied. Then he turned to Emily Grimshaw.

"What's the idea of this upstart in your office? Getting old, eh? Work too much for you?"

"If you bring in any more of this stuff," the agent retorted, "it will be too much for both of us. This girl is clever. She's the only person I ever met who can revise your sister's poetry as well as I can."

Now Jasper Crosby's hawk eyes were fixed on Judy. He studied her for a moment while she met his gaze unflinchingly.

"Huh!" he grunted. "Watch your step, now. It takes queer people to revise queer poetry, and, mind you, this stuff has got to sell. Bring it out in book form. Jazz it up! Make it popular, and the public will eat it. That so, cutie?" He gave Judy's cheek a playful pinch as he turned to leave.

"The nerve of him!" she expostulated. "He's the most repulsive person I have ever seen."

"Quite so," the agent agreed. "Quite so and, strange to say, his sister was once the most charming. You can see it yet in some of her verses. I would be more enthusiastic about this book of her collected poems if I had any assurance that the royalties would go to her."

"Why won't they?" Judy asked.

"Because he tells me that her health is failing. Years ago I was witness to her will, and the entire estate goes to that scoundrel, Jasper Crosby."

As Judy busied herself typing and correcting the poetry this thought kept recurring to her mind. Nevertheless, the work itself fascinated her. She conceived the idea of grouping the verses with a sub-title for each group. Miss Grimshaw beamed her pleasure.

"A fine idea, Miss Bolton, a really constructive idea. It will take considerable time but don't try to hurry. Better keep the manuscripts on your own desk and have the thing done right."

"Could I take them home?" Judy ventured the question and immediately wished she had not asked it.

The agent's eyes snapped. "Indeed not! Don't you realize, young lady, that original manuscripts are sometimes very valuable? This poet is well known, and plenty of people would be glad to buy them or, what's worse, steal them."

Judy had not considered this. It had simply

occurred to her that Irene might help arrange the poems. She liked to hear her read in her low, musical voice. She would make the poems live and catch hidden meanings between the lines. Judy tried to explain all this to her employer. She felt that she must excuse her own thoughtlessness.

"Well, if you are so anxious to have your friend help you, bring her here," the old lady said with a sudden show of generosity.

Irene was thrilled when Judy told her.

"I feel as if this is a real occasion and I ought to dress up for it," she declared. "A package came this morning from Farringdon, and I've been suspecting all the time that it's a new dress. My birthday isn't for another week, but do you think Dad would mind if I opened my present now?"

Without waiting for a reply, Irene ran to get the box her father had labeled, *For My Little Girl's Seventeenth Birthday*. When she pulled off the wrappings the folds of a shimmering yellow satin dress fell into her hands. She stood up, holding it for Judy and Pauline to admire.

"Gorgeous!" Judy exclaimed. "Look at the

puffed sleeves and high waistline! Why, it's the very newest thing!"

"But it's a party dress," Pauline objected. "Really, it's not at all the thing to wear in Emily Grimshaw's office."

"For once," Irene announced, "I'm going to wear exactly what I want to wear whether it's proper or not."

Judy smiled at her independence. She had often felt that way herself. After all, what difference did it make? And Irene was breath takingly lovely in the new dress. She stood before the long mirror in Pauline's room while Judy pinned her hair in soft, bright curls at the back of her neck. Then she walked back a little distance, surveying the effect.

"You're beautiful!" Judy exclaimed. "That dress fits in with your complexion as though you were part of a picture. You're prettier than Lois or Honey or Lorraine. Don't you think so, Pauline?"

She admitted it.

"Prettier than Lorraine?" Irene repeated wonderingly. Lorraine Lee had always considered herself the prettiest girl in Farringdon and dressed accordingly, while Irene's faded

blues and browns had never flattered her.  But
in the new yellow dress she was transformed.
There was a tiny jacket to go with it, also of
yellow but more delicately golden, matching
slippers and, in the very bottom of the box, a
gold locket.  Irene, delighting in her own reck-
lessness, wore them all the next morning.

# CHAPTER VII

EMILY GRIMSHAW often came in late, but as Judy had her own key this affected her work very little. In fact, she usually accomplished more when alone. Thus she was not surprised to find the office vacant when she and Irene arrived.

"It's every bit as queer as you said it was," Irene whispered as they unlocked the door and she examined the brass knocker. "She must trust you, Judy." She smiled into her friend's honest gray eyes. "And who wouldn't?"

The girls seated themselves at either end of the long sofa in Emily Grimshaw's office. With the pile of handwritten poetry between them it was easier to help each other decide into which group certain verses belonged.

"Some of them are rather horrible," Judy remarked as she hunted through the pile. "I'll sort out the worst ones, and you can read the others."

46

"Oh, no! Let me read the horrible ones," Irene begged.

Judy laughed. "Everyone to his own notions. I don't mind, if you feel like giving yourself the shivers."

There was a long table just back of the sofa, and it came in handy for the completed groups of papers. Judy removed a vase of flowers and a few books and made a clear place for the different piles.

"*Golden Girl* goes at the top of the list," she remarked, as she took a yellowed slip of paper in her hand. "Miss Grimshaw says it's valuable."

"Is it the song?"

"It is," Judy replied. "This poet wrote it. Imagine! And then turns to such morbid things as that one I fixed up; you remember, about the tower of flame?"

She broke off suddenly as the telephone on Emily Grimshaw's desk jangled imperiously.

Both girls were buried in papers, and the telephone rang a second time before Judy was free to answer it.

"The switchboard operator says it's Dale Meredith!"

She turned away from the mouthpiece and gave out this information in an excited whisper. Irene let a few of the papers slide to the floor.

"Oh, Judy," she cried, "our scheme did work after all!"

Judy's answer was a glance of triumph, but her voice over the wire sounded very business-like.

"Tell him to come up and wait. Miss Grimshaw will be in shortly."

In the moment before he mounted the stairs Irene had time to smooth her hair and powder her nose. Then she picked up the fallen papers and was about to place them on the table.

"Never mind the work now. I'll straighten things," Judy told her. "You just sit there and look pretty when Dale Meredith comes in."

The handsome young author greeted them with a surprised whistle. "Whoever expected to find you here!" he exclaimed, smiling first at Judy who stood beside the open door and then at Irene. "Why, the place looks like a palace with the princess enthroned on the sofa. What's happened to Her Royal Highness?"

"You mean Miss Grimshaw?" Judy asked, laughing. "She will be in presently."

JUDY PINNED IRENE'S HAIR IN SOFT BRIGHT CURLS
AT THE BACK OF HER NECK.

"Not too 'presently,' I hope," Dale replied, seating himself beside Irene. "Before we talk business I want to hear what happened to you girls. I've been scolding myself ever since for not finding out your names. The truth of the matter is, I was so dog-goned interested in that *Art Shop Robbery*——"

"The title of your new book?" Judy ventured, and his nod told her that she had reasoned correctly.

"You see, it was a rush order," he went on to explain. "There seems to be a big demand for mystery stories. Most people like to imagine themselves as sleuths or big time detectives. I do, myself. The trouble is, there aren't enough mysteries in real life to supply the demand for plots, and what there are make tales too gruesome to be good reading."

"You do write gruesome stories then?" Irene asked anxiously.

He studied her face for a moment before he answered. "That depends on your definition of the word. I never make it a point to dwell on the details of a murder. Suffice it to tell under what circumstances the body was found——"

"Don't talk about it, please! You sound so cold and matter-of-fact, as if you didn't feel it at all. Your flying stories are so different!"

"They were written from first-hand knowledge," he explained. "I had a pilot's license and flew with a friend of mine across the continent. There was story material and plenty of it!" He went on for fifteen minutes discussing his experiences with the girls.

Dale Meredith had a knack of telling stories so that the listeners lived his adventures with him. Judy and Irene sat enthralled. They were both imagining themselves scrambling out of a wrecked plane in their own Allegheny Mountains when the door opened, and in walked Emily Grimshaw! Dale and Judy both greeted her, but when Irene looked up and smiled the old lady started back as if she had seen a ghost. Judy, thinking she must be ill, helped her into a chair.

"Is there anything I can do?" she asked solicitously.

"There's a bottle." Emily Grimshaw made a gesture with her hand. "Pour me out a bit. I need a stimulant. I must be getting old. Good lord! I must be seeing things!"

She took the glass that Judy held out to her and swallowed the contents in three great gulps, then rubbed her eyes and looked at Irene again.

"Guess the stuff is too strong," she muttered and slumped in her chair.

Irene clutched Dale's arm. "She isn't going to die?" she asked in a panicky whisper.

More than a little bewildered, the young man reassured her and suggested that she wait downstairs in the lobby.

"She seems to have affected Miss Grimshaw strangely," he explained to Judy later.

"Yes, and Irene can't stand too much excitement," she returned. "You didn't know, but for the past three years she's been working almost day and night, taking care of her crippled father. She'd be doing it yet if my dad hadn't arranged to have him cared for in a sanitarium. It's better for him and better for Irene. Her mother is dead."

"Poor kid! No wonder she thought something dreadful had happened to Her Majesty."

Judy had gone for a pitcher of water and stood beside her employer's chair dampening her handkerchief and rubbing her forehead.

That seemed to have little effect, but when Dale attempted to move her to the sofa the old lady promptly opened her eyes and protested violently. She staggered back to her chair and sat there staring at the spot where Irene had sat. Then she sighed heavily. "Old fool that I am—seeing things."

# CHAPTER VIII

### THE MISSING POEMS

THE agent's collapse had unnerved Judy more than a little, and it was some time before she settled herself to her work. Dale had left but not before promising to see Irene safely home.

"She probably won't want to come near the office again," Judy thought. "Poor Irene! I wonder what made Emily Grimshaw act up and scare her so."

But this was no time for deductions, Judy knew, when so much work remained to be done —twice as much now. And there was no use sitting in comfort on the sofa, either. Alone, she could group the poems better at her own desk.

She lowered the typewriter until a place was clear above it and then went for the pile of manuscripts. She looked on the table back of the sofa, but they were not there.

"That's queer," she thought. "I'm sure we

left them right on the corner of that table. I
saw Irene when she put *Golden Girl* back, and
it was right on top. But maybe she moved
them afterwards.''

Next Judy looked on the sofa and under all
three cushions. She felt beneath the arms, then
got down on her hands and knees and looked
under the sofa on the floor. She even lifted
the rug and looked under that.

"What *are* you doing?" Emily Grimshaw inquired, looking up with a scowl.

"Hunting for something," Judy answered
vaguely. She was not ready to tell her employer that the manuscripts were missing, not
after having been told how valuable they were.
Perhaps, absent-mindedly she had placed them
in one of the drawers of her own desk.

After another ten minutes of Judy's frantic
searching the agent's patience was exhausted.

"Sit down, young lady, and tell me why you
are turning my office upside down in this ridiculous fashion. As if I hadn't enough worries!"

"I'm sorry, Miss Grimshaw," Judy replied
contritely. "But the poems you gave me—the
originals, I mean—they seem to have—disappeared.''

"Disappeared! Stuff and nonsense!" the old lady snorted. "Like all girls, you've been careless, and misplaced them."

"I've looked everywhere except in your desk, and they couldn't be there."

"They couldn't, eh? We shall see."

Soon the agent had her own desk in worse confusion than Judy's, but no papers could she find. She poured herself another drink from the bottle and regarded Judy with a wild light in her eyes.

"Joy Holiday took them! That's what happened! I knew that girl was here for a reason."

After that there was a long silence during which Emily Grimshaw sat moving her lips but making no sound. It was uncanny! Judy longed for five o'clock and freedom from her queer employer.

No one had entered the office; of that Judy felt sure. The sofa was opposite the door. No one could have passed it and taken the pile of papers from the table without being seen. And no one could enter without a key. The door locked from the inside, and Judy never left the catch off except when Emily Grimshaw was there. That had been her employer's instructions, and she had followed them to the letter.

What, then, could she mean by saying Joy Holiday took the poems? Why had she collapsed the moment Irene looked up at her, and who or what had taken the pile of manuscripts?

Judy shivered. Would it be stretching the truth to say that some strange, invisible force had been at work in the office that day? Irene, timid, lovable little girl that she was, couldn't possibly frighten a big capable woman like Emily Grimshaw. She must have seen something else!

Without meaning to, Judy glanced over her shoulder. Then a thought came to her that seemed all at once amusing. Dale Meredith had said there weren't enough mysteries in real life. Wait till she told him this one! A writer of detective stories ought to be interested. He might even have a theory, perhaps from his own novels, that would work out a solution.

Or perhaps Dale knew what had happened to the poetry. He didn't seem dishonest, but if he refused to show an interest or showed too great an interest . . . How was it that people told the guilty party?

These questions ran through Judy's mind as she sat before her typewriter. Mysteries intrigued her. But no mystery on earth would be worth the solving if it lessened her trust in people she loved.

"There has to be some way to get Irene out of this," she said to herself. "Whatever Emily Grimshaw saw, she mustn't be allowed to accuse Irene of taking the poetry."

Then it occurred to Judy that, ordinarily, she would be under suspicion as well. Instead, Emily Grimshaw suspected someone named Joy Holiday. It sounded like an hallucination.

When closing time came, Judy walked in the direction of Gramercy Park and arrived at Dr. Faulkner's house just as Pauline was leaving through a side door.

"Where are you going?" Judy asked in surprise. Usually Pauline would not be going out just at dinner time.

"I told Mary I'd not be home," Pauline replied, "and you had better not be, either. Dale Meredith's up on the roof garden with Irene, and we would be intruding if we thrust ourselves upon them."

"Why? What makes you think that?"

"Just what I overheard."

"Perhaps you didn't understand," Judy attempted. "There's a brand-new mystery for us to solve. I'm sure Dale Meredith wants to hear about it. Something happened in the office today, and Irene was dreadfully upset. He may have been trying to comfort her."

Pauline laughed bitterly. "A queer way of doing it—calling her a sweet girl, holding her hand and saying something about 'another roof garden . . . peppy orchestra, floor as smooth as wax . . . and you to dance with . . .' He said more, too, but that was all I heard. You see what a mistake I almost made! Of course he wants Irene to himself. He won't be interested in your mystery now—only in Irene's glorious eyes and her bright hair. I guess she knew what she was doing when she wore that party dress."

"You wouldn't feel that way if you knew how little pleasure Irene has had in her life," Judy said. "My brother is the only boy who ever paid any attention to her, and he never took her out alone."

"That doesn't excuse her for dolling up on purpose to attract Dale Meredith."

"Why, she didn't even know he was going to come into the office! She dressed up only because it pleased her to look pretty. It pleased me, too," Judy added warmly. "Do you think they have really gone out together, Pauline?"

"I'm sure of it. And she doesn't deserve it after scheming to meet him. I'll never quite forgive her, and you're a little bit to blame, too. It wasn't just the thing to go off and find yourself a position when you are really my guest."

"I suppose it wasn't," Judy admitted, feeling sorry for Pauline in spite of the attitude she had taken. She couldn't be blamed too much. It promised to be another one of these eternal triangles. Judy thought of Peter Dobbs and Arthur Farringdon-Pett at home. They both liked her and were still good friends to each other. She thought of Horace and Honey and Irene. One triangle made straight, only to be converted into another and more puzzling one. Why couldn't Dale Meredith take out both Pauline and Irene, she wondered. She would even be willing to tag along if it would help. But tonight she would tag along with Pauline and sympathize.

They had hot chocolate and sandwiches in a

drug store and called it their dinner. After that they walked uptown as far as Central Park and then back again in time to see the last show at a near-by movie.

"No need to hurry," Judy said. "Irene is sure to be home late if she and Dale Meredith went out to dance."

# CHAPTER IX

IT WAS twelve o'clock when Judy and Pauline, her head held high, walked into the house. All the lights were on and the radio was going in Pauline's parlor room, but, as no one was there, they went on through to the roof garden. Irene looked up from the hammock.

"Oh, there you are!" she exclaimed. "Dale and I have been so worried. We couldn't imagine where you were."

Pauline noticed the familiar use of his first name and winced. The young author had been sitting beside Irene, and now he rose and stood smiling. Again Pauline felt as if she wanted to run away, but this time it was impossible.

Judy excused their lateness as well as she could without telling them she expected that they would be dancing. Irene soon explained that.

"You missed the most wonderful time," she said. "Dale was going to take us to a hotel roof garden to dance, but when you didn't come in we had to wait."

"You could have left a note," Pauline replied. "I'm sorry to have spoiled your date."

"It isn't spoiled," Dale returned. "With your consent, we are going tomorrow night."

"Why *with my consent?* Irene is old enough to take care of herself."

"But can't you see?" he protested. "I want all three of you to come."

"You can leave me out."

"Why, Pauline," Irene exclaimed, "I thought——"

"Never mind what you thought," Judy interrupted. She knew that Irene had been about to say she thought Pauline wanted to meet interesting people. Then Dale would know she thought him interesting, and that wouldn't be a very good thing to reveal right then. But Judy spoke more sharply than she realized, and her tone held the smallest hint of suspicion.

Irene's expressive eyes were dark with reproach. "Judy!" she cried, almost in tears, "Now what have I done to offend you?"

"Nothing, dear. Nothing at all. I'm just tired."

"You must be tired," Dale put in. "Who wouldn't be, after such a hectic day? But why take it out on Irene? She isn't to blame if Her Majesty makes a grouch of herself."

"Of course not," Judy agreed, not quite sure that she spoke the truth. Certainly Irene *had* had something to do with Emily Grimshaw's grouch for the old lady had not been herself since the moment she set eyes on the dainty figure in yellow, curled on her sofa in the office that morning.

"You don't know the half of it," she went on to explain. "Her Majesty, as you call her, acted queer and talked to herself like a crazy person all day. I didn't dare speak to her for fear she'd go off in a fit again. She thinks someone, or something, came into the office. Did you ever hear of a person named Joy Holiday?"

"No, never," Dale replied.

Then Judy turned to Irene. "Did you?"

"You know I didn't," she replied in surprise. "Why, Judy, you know everyone I know at home, and I have no friends here except Pauline. Why do you ask?"

"Because Emily Grimshaw thinks someone

It was the same portfolio that he had carried on the bus, the same portfolio that he had taken away with him when he left Emily Grimshaw's office. Now Judy remembered watching Dale and Irene from the office window as they walked through Madison Square. Irene had carried nothing except her brown hand bag. That was far too small to hold the manuscript. But Dale's portfolio— Why, even now it bulged with papers that must be inside! Yes, Judy had to face it, Dale Meredith might have taken the poems. They might be inside that very portfolio!

Excusing herself, she went inside. Blackberry followed at her heels.

# CHAPTER X

## DEDUCTIONS

TORN between a desire to find out what had actually happened and a fear of throwing suspicion upon the man who was Irene's ideal, Judy stood in the center of the room staring at Dale Meredith's portfolio. Blackberry sat on the floor at her feet, and the thumping of his tail on the rug played a drumlike march in time to her heartbeats. This was nonsense—just standing there. It was her duty to find out the truth.

She took a quick step forward and reached for the portfolio, accidentally stepping on the cat's tail. He yowled! Judy almost dropped the papers that she held, caught at them, told in one glance that she had been wrong and was about to put them back when the door slowly opened.

There was no way out. Dale and the two girls came into the room, stopped and stood speechless. Blackberry looked up at them as though expecting to be commended for sounding the warning.

"That cat's as good as a watchdog," Dale broke the silence by saying.

"I suppose I do look something like a burglar," Judy retorted. "I'm not going to apologize for anything either. I simply had to know."

"Know what?" Pauline asked.

"She wanted to find out if I took the lost poetry," Dale explained. "That's clear enough, and don't think for a moment that I blame her. Any good detective would have done the same thing. Being a comparative stranger, I am the logical one to suspect. Irene, we all know, is above suspicion."

"Well then, who did take the papers?" Pauline asked.

Dale only shook his head, refusing to propound any more theories about the affair. Judy turned to him gratefully.

"I felt sure you would be dreadfully mad at me for snooping in your personal belongings," she said. "It's nice to have you uphold me in my crude bit of detecting, and I do appreciate it. What puzzles me is this: nobody left the room ahead of you except——"

"Except me," Irene broke in, "and you may be sure I didn't take those papers."

"We're sure, aren't we?"

Judy turned to the others and Dale nodded solemnly. It was Pauline who looked a little doubtful.

"What! Don't you believe in her too?" Judy asked in surprise.

Pauline shrugged. "I suppose so, if she says she didn't take them."

"Then we all believe in each other, and it seems that even Emily Grimshaw believes in us," Judy went on. "It appears that the next thing to do is find out who Joy Holiday is and how she could have entered the office without our knowing."

"You're pretty keen on solving this mystery, aren't you?" Dale inquired.

"It's just the way I am," Judy replied. "I couldn't bear not knowing. And I suspect that this Joy Holiday, whoever she is, had something to do with Miss Grimshaw's collapse.

Maybe tomorrow, if she's in a pleasant mood, I'll ask her about it."

"Go easy," Dale warned. "I'm beginning to think there's more to this missing poetry business than may appear on the surface. What were they—very valuable manuscripts?"

"Valuable?" Judy repeated thoughtfully. "Why, I believe they were."

"There was *Golden Girl*," Irene put in. "You said that was valuable. It's beautiful, too. I read it over and over and over——"

"You're getting sleepy, Irene. And no wonder!" Pauline looked at her wrist watch a second time to make sure. Then she turned to Dale. "One o'clock! Oh, what a calling down I'll get from Father if the housekeeper catches sight of you leaving at this hour of the night. Better tiptoe down the back stairs."

"Okay! How about that roof garden tomorrow night?"

"Not tomorrow night," Irene pleaded. "I'll be too tired. Can't we wait?"

"Saturday, then. How about it, Pauline?"

"I said I wasn't going."

"But you must go. We won't go without her, will we, Irene?"

She shook her bright head and laughed, "Indeed we won't. Don't be a goose!"

Did they want her, too, Judy wondered. Then she thought of Emily Grimshaw, and her doubts vanished. She might have something interesting to tell them about Joy Holiday.

# CHAPTER XI

SATURDAY night came, and when Dale Meredith called, three visions of loveliness awaited
him.  Pauline wore peach-colored satin that
trailed nearly to the floor.  Irene's new yellow
dress with matching slippers of gold was truly
appropriate for this occasion, and Judy looked
like a sea nymph in a pale shade of green that
made people wonder about the color of her
eyes.

"It's going to be a perfect evening," Irene
sighed ecstatically.  "Even the moon came out
to shine on the roof garden."

It was all that Dale had described—palms,
cut flowers, waiters in long-tailed coats who
moved noiselessly between the tables, and a
circle of floor for dancing. Colored lights played
on the dancers tinting them with rainbows.  To
her surprise, Dale asked Judy for the first
dance.

"Oh, no," she replied quickly.  "Really, I'd

rather you danced with the other girls. You
see, I can watch the lights while I'm sitting
here. When I'm home again I won't be able to
watch lights on a roof garden. And I can always dance.''

Afterwards Judy felt almost sorry she had
refused. The orchestra was playing beauti-
fully, magic to any young girl's feet. Now and
then a soloist would sing the number as it was
played. Judy listened, at first watching Dale
and Irene, then Dale and Pauline as they moved
in and out among the crowd of dancers.
Finally, not watching anybody, she just sat
thinking.

It had been a queer day. Strangely enough,
Emily Grimshaw had not once mentioned the
missing poetry. She seemed to take it for
granted that neither Dale nor Judy were responsible. But she had gone about her work
with a harassed expression and a droop to her
shoulders that Judy had never noticed before.
An opportunity came, and she had asked about
Joy Holiday. She had found out something,
too, and now as she sat alone at the table she
puzzled as how best to tell Dale Meredith. At
first she had planned to tell Irene but, on second

thought, she had decided that it might be better for Irene not to know some of the things Emily Grimshaw had said.

"You must dance this one," Dale urged her as the music began again. "Pauline is dancing with a friend of mine who just came in——"

"And I haven't had a chance to finish this ginger ale," Irene added.

Dale was curious to hear what she had found out. Judy could tell that as soon as he spoke to her alone.

"Her Majesty's grouch gone?" he asked.

"A sort of depression has taken its place," Judy explained as she swung into step. The floor was like glass and shone with their reflections. She could see Irene sitting next to the circle of light, sipping her ginger ale. There was another girl reflected on the floor beside her. Judy pointed it out to Dale—that golden reflection on the polished floor.

Just then the orchestra struck up a new tune. Soon the soloist joined in, singing the latest popular song:

My own golden girl, there is one. only one,
Who has eyes like the stars and hair like the
    sun.

In your new yellow gown you're a dream of
delight.
You have danced in my heart on bright
slippers tonight . . .

"It sounds as if he meant Irene," Dale whispered. "She's a 'golden girl' tonight." He glanced again at her reflection as the orchestra played on:

I'll enthrone you my queen in a circular tower
Where frost may not blight my most delicate
flower.
And from this hour on, you belong all to me
Though you drown in my love as a bird in the
sea.

Irene looked up just as the music stopped. She smiled, and Dale's eyes smiled back at her.

"Her hair is like the sun," he said dreamily and half to himself.

"Yes," Judy replied. "And her dress and slippers are golden. You'd almost think the song was written for her. It must have been written for someone very much like her, and whoever wrote it loved that someone dearly."

"What was the poet's name?" Dale asked.

Judy thought a minute. "It was Sarah Glynn—or Glenn. I don't quite remember. I used to think the song was written by a man until Miss Grimshaw showed me the original manuscript. It's one of the missing poems, you know.''

"And you didn't find out a thing about it?''

"Yes, one thing.''

Dale's face glowed with interest. "You did? What?''

"That Emily Grimshaw believes Irene's name is Joy Holiday. I can't convince her otherwise. And she is sure Joy Holiday took the poems. You know it's ridiculous. Irene isn't anybody but herself and wouldn't have any use in the world for the faded old poetry. Besides, she said she didn't take them, and I believe her.''

"Keep on believing her,'' Dale advised as he ushered Judy back to the table. "My own opinion is that your beloved employer has worked a screw loose somewhere in her upper story.''

Judy giggled, partly from excitement. But the thought would be less entertaining when she was catering to the old lady's whims at the office.

On the way home they discussed the mystery. When questioned, Irene seemed glad to contribute scraps of the missing poetry for the others to puzzle over. It was remarkable how much of it she remembered, and Dale was charmed with the soft tones of her voice as she recited.

When the word "Joy" came up for the fifth time Judy stopped her to exclaim, "That must mean Joy Holiday, the girl Emily Grimshaw thinks took the poetry."

"Then she must have been 'Golden Girl,' " Irene said unexpectedly.

Dale turned to her in surprise. "That's right! We never thought of that. I'm glad to see you so interested in it; I thought at first you weren't keen on detecting."

"I'm not," Irene admitted. "It's the poetry I like."

Judy shuddered. "Those creepy poems! I'd rather read a good murder mystery any day. At least there's always a solution. What do you suppose this poet means when she says 'Better to crumble in a tower of flame than sit with ghosts . . .'? Could the ghosts be memories, too?"

"They could be," Irene said thoughtfully. "It's queer, but *Golden Girl* mentions a tower."

"So it does!" Dale exclaimed, growing excited. "It looks as though there might be some connection. Do you know, girls, we may find the solution to this whole mystery in that poetry!"

"I have some of the typewritten copies. I'll hunt through them for clues," Judy promised.

# CHAPTER XII

UNEXPECTEDLY, the next day Jasper Crosby came into the office with another lot of his sister's poems. This time they were in a tin box with padlock attached.

Judy listened in silence as the earlier manuscripts were discussed, wondering how Emily Grimshaw would break the news of their disappearance. Presently she realized that the poet's brother was being kept in ignorance of the whole affair. Worse than that, he was being deceived. What did the agent mean by saying the publishers were considering Sarah Glenn's work?

Thinking there might be some mistake, Judy refrained from asking questions until she and her employer were alone again. Then she expressed herself frankly.

"It isn't right," she declared, "not to tell him the truth about those poems. We can't publish them when they're lost."

"Tut, tut, child," Miss Grimshaw reproved in a patronizing tone that always annoyed Judy. "You must never correct your elders. Haven't you heard that there are tricks to all trades?"

"Not dishonest tricks." Judy's scruples about deceit and treachery had made her overbold.

"Look here, Miss Bolton," her employer cried. "If this position means anything to you, learn to keep a civil tongue in your head. I have evidence enough against you right now to place the blame on your shoulders if I wanted to. The idea! Talking about dishonest tricks! Wasn't it a dishonest trick that somebody played on me?"

"Yes, Miss Grimshaw," Judy answered penitently. "I shouldn't have spoken so hastily, and if you blame me . . ."

"But I don't blame you, child. You're as innocent as I am. That's why I hired you—because I knew I could trust you."

This unexpected praise brought a flood of color to Judy's cheeks. She mumbled something intended for an acknowledgment. Not hearing the interruption, her employer went on talking.

THERE WAS ANOTHER GIRL REFLECTED ON
THE FLOOR.

"I know we can't keep putting Jasper Crosby off forever, but, don't you see, we must do it until the poems are found? I'm ruined if we don't."

"I suppose he would hold you responsible," Judy ventured.

"He would exactly," the agent declared. "He'd charge me with gross negligence or something of the kind and sue me for more money than Sarah Glenn's royalties would bring in a lifetime. He's just crooked enough to get away with it. And," she finished tragically, "all our time and work will go for nothing. Oh, Miss Bolton, if you can help me, won't you do it? You're clever. Perhaps you can figure it out. My mind gets all befuddled of late—ever since Joy Holiday came back. Find her. She's got the papers."

"I'll do my best," Judy promised, genuinely moved. She resolved to tackle this new task her employer had given her with all the seriousness it demanded. But whom was there to suspect? Joy Holiday, as far as she could figure out, was a creature of Miss Grimshaw's imagination, a ghost. Judy refused to believe in ghosts or be frightened by them. That angle of the mystery she dismissed as wholly implausible. She had proved Dale Meredith's innocence to her own satisfaction, and Irene hadn't taken the poetry. Judy felt sure of that.

She was still sure the following Thursday when she and Pauline planned a birthday party for her. Dale happened to come in the office, and Judy told him. Together they arranged a surprise dinner. At first he wanted to take them to an exclusive restaurant but was soon won over when Judy suggested a meal served out on the roof garden. Pauline liked the idea, too, and found a great deal of pleasure in planning the menu. She telephoned to the market and ordered a good-sized capon; nuts, celery and raisins were to go into the dressing. There would be fruit cups and salads, and ice cream for dessert and, of course, a cake with candles. Judy came home early to make the cake. While Pauline helped Mary put on the roast she continued fixing things, waiting for Dale who expected to arrive ahead of Irene.

"It looks great!" he exclaimed as soon as he opened the door and saw the table set in the center of the roof garden. It was decorated with yellow candy cups and tall yellow candles.

"And isn't it lucky that I brought yellow flowers?"

"You knew we'd be decorating in yellow," Pauline charged as she took the flowers and buried her face in their fragrance. Then, while Dale stood admiring the tasteful arrangement of the table, she placed them as an appropriate centerpiece. Everything was ready, and it was after six o'clock.

"Irene ought to be here," Judy said anxiously. "I wonder where she went."

Pauline had seen her go out early that morning, carrying a borrowed book.

"She'd stop in on her way home to return it. Dale, why don't you and Judy go down to the bookstore and meet her?"

"Can't you leave the dinner long enough to come with us?"

Pauline laughed. "I guess I could if you want me. There's a chance of missing her, though. She may come from another direction."

Dale helped Judy and Pauline with their wraps, and together they walked toward the bookstore. It was only a short distance, but the cool air felt good to Judy after having spent all afternoon over the cake. As they walked they watched for Irene. She would be wearing a brown suit with a close-fitting brown hat to match, Pauline said. The outfit was new and she wondered if, for that reason, they had missed her.

At the bookstore, however, the girl who took care of lending out books from the circulating library told them that Miss Lang had not been in since morning when she returned a book.

"What could have happened to her?" Judy exclaimed in real concern.

"Perhaps she went out shopping to celebrate. I've seen girls shop before. They never leave the stores until closing time."

"It's closing time now."

"And she'll probably be waiting for us back at the house," Dale prophesied cheerfully.

"Oh," exclaimed Judy, "I hope she doesn't peek in the ice box and see her cake. I do believe I forgot to put Blackberry out, and if he smells that chicken . . ." She finished the sentence with a gesture of hopelessness.

Blackberry was out—out on the roof garden —when they returned. Sensing a party in the air, he had taken advantage of his mistress' absence and upset the vase of yellow flowers.

There were bits of chewed flower petals and ferns scattered all about.

"You bad cat!" cried Judy, shaking him. "Just look what he's done. And Irene isn't here yet! Let's hurry and put the place in order before she comes. Collect the flowers, Dale, won't you? I think I can save a few of these ferns."

She was on her knees, hunting for pieces of them as she spoke.

"And I'll get Mary to wipe up the water and put on a clean cloth," Pauline offered.

Soon everything was in order again.

Oliver had hung a string of Japanese lanterns all the way across the roof garden. They were a little too low, and for a few more minutes Dale and the girls busied themselves with a pole, raising them to a higher level.

Meanwhile it had grown dark, and Judy suggested lighting the candles on the table so that Irene would see them the moment she opened the door. Then they planned to call out, "Surprise!" all at once. Judy could imagine the rest—Irene laughing, exclaiming, her two eyes like stars as she enjoyed her very first birthday party.

In the kitchen below a sizzling noise called Mary to the oven. The roast needed basting again. It was too brown already, but she couldn't take it off and let it get cold. The potatoes had cracked open and their jackets were done to a crisp. She turned the flame as low as she dared and faced about to see Dale and the girls standing in the doorway.

"Getting hungry?" she asked.

"A little. Irene ought to be here by now."

"I know it," the housekeeper replied, "and the dinner will be spoiled if we let it wait much longer."

# CHAPTER XIII

## WAITING

EIGHT o'clock came and still no Irene. By nine o'clock Judy was in tears. She felt that something dreadful must have happened and suggested calling up hospitals to see if there had been any accidents. After the calls were completed Dale returned to the kitchen and stood looking at the dinner.

"You might as well eat some of the chicken," Mary suggested. She placed it on a platter and carried it up to the roof garden, but they ate only a little, cut from underneath where it wouldn't show. Then they left the table as it was, waiting for Irene.

The yellow candles burned lower and lower. Finally they flickered and went out. Pauline gave a little start, but Judy sank back in her chair shaking with sobs.

"I—I'm not superstitious," she blurted out. "I'm trying to be sensible about it, but do you think it's sensible just to wait?"

87

"There isn't anything else to do unless we notify the police, and then, if she had just been to a movie, wouldn't she have the laugh on us?"

"But, Pauline, she isn't thoughtless."

"I could tell that," Dale put in seriously. "She's a mighty fine little girl. I know how you feel, Judy. I'll stand by. Didn't Irene and I wait up that night for you—and nothing had happened except that you took a walk?"

Dale was comforting. It was nice to have him there, especially when Judy knew that he was as interested as she in Irene's safe return. But Judy could not help thinking of Farringdon and the enthusiasm with which the boys there would help her if they only knew.

Pauline thought of Farringdon too.

"Maybe Irene didn't like it here in New York and went home," she suggested.

"But the house is empty," Judy objected. "There really isn't any home in Farringdon for her to go back to. She doesn't even know where they are going to live when her father is well again. He's in a sanitarium now, and I hate to notify him if there's any other way. It really would be better to notify the police."

"I guess you're right," Dale agreed. "If she isn't home by midnight we might try it. Things do happen—and especially to pretty girls," he added gravely.

It was five minutes to twelve when footsteps were finally heard outside the door. Dale started to his feet, and Judy rushed toward the door, then halted with a cry of disappointment as she recognized the now familiar, "Hit's Oliver, Miss."

Pauline opened the door and urged him to come in.

"Irene isn't home yet, and Mr. Meredith was waiting," she explained. "Did you happen to see her?"

"Well, let me think a minute." The English servant passed his fingers through his thinning hair. "Indeed, yes, Miss Pauline, I did see her when the post came this morning. She stood hin the vestibule reading a letter."

"Did she seem worried, as if it were bad news?"

The man shook his head. "Indeed, she seemed quite 'appy over hit. She went out a bit later 'umming a tune, 'De de-de da de. Da de da. Da de dum'—like that."

He had given a crude imitation of the first notes of *Golden Girl*.

"She was very fond of that song," Dale remarked after Oliver had left. He was helping the girls with their wraps preparatory to calling at the police station.

Again Judy thought about the papers. Could their disappearance and Irene's, in some way, be connected? She mentioned the possibility to Dale but he thought it unlikely.

"At any rate we know Irene didn't take them, and when we make our report to the police we had better leave the papers entirely out of it."

"And the name 'Joy Holiday'?" Pauline questioned.

"Yes, for the present. We want to do all we can to save her from embarrassment until we have an explanation. I feel sure that, whatever it is, it will be—like Irene—satisfactory."

"I'm glad you believe in her, Dale," Judy said. She hoped, with all her heart, that Irene would prove herself worthy of his loyalty.

At the police station the sergeant on night duty at the desk did not take their story very seriously. He had a great many such cases, he explained, most of which solved themselves.

His questions, however, suggested terrifying possibilities. Did she have any enemies, any rejected suitors, any hostile relatives? Was she wearing any valuable jewels? How much money did she have in her purse?

Judy thought it was about ten dollars.

"Ten dollars could take that girl a long way," the officer said significantly. "What about publicity on the case? We broadcast a general alarm for missing persons every evening over the radio."

Undecided, the girls appealed to Dale. "What do you think?"

"That's another day. If she's not home by then, by all means, yes. Anything to find her."

"We'll do our best for you. I'll assign the case to the Detective Bureau right away, but be sure and telephone at once when she comes home. And take my word for it, she'll show up before morning," the sergeant prophesied as they turned to go.

"He probably thinks she's only out on a party," Pauline said later.

"But he doesn't know Irene," Judy reminded her. "She's not the kind of girl police officers are used to dealing with."

"You bet she isn't," Dale agreed fervently.
He promised to be back as soon as it was day-
light and urged the girls to try and get a little
rest in the meantime.  Judy surprised him a
few hours later by announcing that she intended
to spend the day at the office.

"Emily Grimshaw may know something
about this," she explained.  "At least I intend
to find out all there is to know about this Joy
Holiday person.  If there really is someone
who looks exactly like Irene it might get her
into a good deal of trouble."

# CHAPTER XIV

### THE IMMORTAL JOY HOLIDAY

"THAT's a good idea of yours," Dale told Judy just before she left to go to the office. "Have a nice long talk with Her Majesty and I'll meet you at noon to see what she says. In the meantime I'll make some more inquiries at the bookstore and of people in the neighborhood."

"Oh, and you might tell them at the police station that we gave a wrong description of Irene's clothes," Pauline called out to them. She had just been to the closet for her hat and school books and had discovered Irene's brown suit hanging there. Only the yellow dress and jacket were missing from her wardrobe.

"It was the same yellow dress that she wore to the dance," Judy explained.

"And she wore it that day I discovered you in the office," Dale remembered. "She cer-

tainly looked like the heroine of our popular
song then.  Do you suppose there is a chance
that *Golden Girl* was written for her?"

Both girls laughed.  "Dale Meredith!  How
absurd!  It was written twenty years ago."

But when Emily Grimshaw heard of Irene's
disappearance and made a similar suggestion
Judy took it more seriously.  She strained her
ears to hear every word the agent said as she
rocked back and forth in her swivel chair.  Apparently she was talking to herself—something
about the spirit world and Joy's song over the
radio.

"Yes," she went on in a louder tone, "those
poems were written for Joy, every last one of
them, and she sat right on that sofa while I
read *Golden Girl* aloud.  That was twenty years
ago.  Then all of a sudden I see her again after
I think she's dead—same starry eyes, same
golden hair, everything the same, even to her
dress.  Then her mother's poems turn up
missing——"

"So the poet was Joy Holiday's mother!"
Judy interrupted to exclaim.

"Bless you, yes," her employer returned.
"I thought you knew.  She went stark crazy.

Set fire to her own house and tried to burn herself alive.''

''Who did? The poet? How terrible!'' Judy cried, starting from her chair. ''Why, it seems impossible that I've been correcting a crazy woman's verses without even knowing it. Tower of flame, indeed! So that's what she meant!''

Emily Grimshaw laughed dryly. ''Don't ask me what she meant! I'm no authority on crazy people. The asylum's the place for them, and, if it weren't for that mercenary brother of hers, Sarah Glenn would be there yet. He arranged for her release and managed to get himself appointed as her guardian. Handles all of her finances, you see, and takes care of the estate. The poet's pretty much of a recluse. I haven't seen her for years.''

This was beginning to sound more like sense. Hopefully, Judy ventured, ''But you have seen her daughter?''

''Seen her! Seen her!'' she cried. ''That's just it. I see her in my dreams. Ordinarily people don't see spirits and that's why it gave me such a turn the other day. And Joy did come back! Her mother said so in the last poem she ever wrote. Jasper brought it in only this morning.''

"He did!'' Judy exclaimed. ''What did you tell him about the missing poetry?''

"Nothing. And I intend to tell him nothing. If it becomes necessary to tell anyone we'll tell the poet herself. Her address is on this envelope. Keep it, Miss Bolton, you may need it. The poem I mentioned is on the other side.''

Judy turned it over and read:

LINES TO ONE WHO HAS DRUNK
FROM THE FOUNTAIN OF YOUTH

Death cannot touch the halo of your hair
Though, like a ghost, you disappear at will.
I knew you'd come in answer to my
    prayer . . .
You, gentle sprite, whom love alone can
    kill . . .

She shivered. "Spooky, isn't it? And,'' she added, ''like all of her poems, utterly impossible.''

"Hmmm, you think so—now. But you'll see. You'll see.'' And the old lady kept on nodding her head as if the gods had given her an uncanny second-sight.

As far as Judy was concerned, the conversation closed right there. She had learned nothing of importance. In fact, she had learned nothing at all except that her employer believed in spirits. Someone, twenty years ago, had probably looked like Irene. But that wouldn't help find Irene now.

# CHAPTER XV

At noon Judy gave Dale and Pauline what little information she had over sandwiches and coffee in a near-by restaurant. Joy Holiday, she told them, disappeared twenty years ago; and Emily Grimshaw's only reason for acting strangely was because she believed Irene to be her ghost.

"If that's the case," Dale declared, "we're simply wasting time questioning her. Irene's father might know something real."

Judy agreed. They telegraphed him at once:

IRENE MISSING SINCE YESTERDAY STOP IS SHE WITH YOU

JUDY

The answer came back early that same afternoon:

DONT WORRY STOP IRENE WITH RELATIVES IN BROOKLYN STOP ADVISED HER IN LETTER TO LOOK THEM UP

TOM LANG

Relief flooded Judy's face. She waved the telegram excitedly and was on the point of telling the news to Emily Grimshaw. Then she decided that she had better not—not yet, at any rate. The papers were still missing even if Irene was safe. It would be better to clear her chum of all suspicion as quickly as possible.

Freed of a measure of worry and suspense, Judy's mind eagerly took up the story of Joy Holiday's strange disappearance. Now that she felt sure it had nothing to do with Irene she could view the tale dispassionately and take it for what it was worth. Still holding to Dale Meredith's theory that valuable clues might be found in the poetry, she questioned Emily Grimshaw.

"Why do you call the girl Joy Holiday when her mother's name was Glenn?"

"That's only a pen name." The agent explained. "Not any prettier than Holiday, is it? But when she had her first poems published Sarah was so anxious to please the publishers that she agreed to use a name that was short enough to be printed across the back of that thin little book. Humph! And now the publishers are just as anxious to please her!"

"What happened to her husband?" Judy asked after a pause.

"Dick Holiday? He left her shortly after their baby was born. Said he'd married a wife, not a nursemaid, and she insisted upon giving all of her time to Joy. When the child finally made a few friends among young folks her own age her mother, in a fit of jealous rage, locked her in the tower."

"What tower?" Judy asked, growing more and more interested.

"It's a circular tower built onto Sarah's house. Joy's room was on the third floor and there's where her mother locked her up. She wanted Joy all to herself. That's what I call mothering a girl to death. Though how Joy died is still something of a puzzle to me."

"Why? What happened to her?"

Emily Grimshaw's expression changed. The lines in her forehead deepened. "I told you she disappeared, vanished completely, just like you say this friend of yours vanished. Some folks think she jumped from a window. How ever it happened, Jasper Crosby identified a body in the morgue as hers. They had a funeral over it and buried it, but her mother declares to this day it wasn't Joy. It didn't look like her. That girl was too beautiful to die and Sarah thinks she floats around bodily, mind you. No doubt you gathered that much from reading the poetry."

"Oh," Judy exclaimed. "That . . ."

"Yes, *that*. But I doubt it." She shook her head gravely and regarded Judy with a fixed stare. "Yes, I very much doubt it. Joy Holiday must be dead. Otherwise her spirit wouldn't be coming back to haunt the earth. But what I've done that she should haunt me, the good Lord knows!"

"Published the poetry, perhaps," Judy suggested wickedly. If Irene's disappearance hadn't been such a serious matter she would have laughed at the old lady's superstitions.

On the way home Judy tried to figure out why Irene had failed to get in touch with her. That Blackberry had chewed up her note as well as the yellow flower petals seemed likely until she talked it over with Pauline.

"A cat chew up paper?" the other girl sniffed. "Why, Judy, only goats do that."

"I know, but Blackberry is an unusual cat. I thought he might——"

"Well, he wouldn't," Pauline interrupted. "You know, yourself, Irene is sometimes thoughtless. She probably didn't leave any note. She never breathed a word about those relatives either, and I think she must have had some reason for not wanting us to know where she was going."

Judy nodded, unconvinced. Irene wasn't that sort. The relatives in Brooklyn might have been a surprise to her also. Judy remembered distinctly Irene's assertion that she didn't know a soul in the city. Her father must have revealed some family history in his letter. Oh, why did telegrams need to be so brief?

Vaguely uneasy about the whole affair, Judy showed the telegram to Dale when he called later in the evening. As he read it his face beamed.

"What more do you want?" he cried. "She's safe! It's all of Heaven to know that much."

In a little while everything would be explained. Irene hadn't intended to worry them. And Dale was right. They should forget everything else and simply be thankful that she was safe.

For a week Judy went about the daily office

routine cheered by the hope that Irene would soon come back. After that doubts began to crowd in. Dale had been calling regularly, helping Pauline entertain even if there remained only one guest to pilot through the never-ending wonders of the world's greatest city. One evening when he called to take them to dinner Judy confided her fears to him.

"I don't trust that telegram," she said in a low voice. "If Irene really is safe why hasn't she written to tell us where she is?"

"I've been wondering about that for a week," Dale replied. "Suppose we send another telegram."

"And have it answered as briefly as the last one? No," Judy declared emphatically. "I'm going to find out what has happened if it costs my week's salary in nickels. Where's the nearest phone booth?"

Dale pointed out a cigar store at the next corner and escorted her to it. Together she and Pauline assembled quite a pile of coins and Judy dropped her first nickel in the slot. It was a relief to hear a nurse's voice, finally, at the other end of the wire.

"Farringdon Sanitarium?" she asked. "Is

Mr. Lang well enough to come to the phone?"

"Oh, yes indeed," the voice replied. "Just a moment and I will call him. He is taking a walk around the grounds."

"He's taking a walk," Judy turned and whispered. "Won't Irene be glad to hear he's out of his wheeled chair?"

Then Mr. Lang's voice, wonderfully clear, asked who was calling.

"It's Judy. I called about Irene."

"About Irene!" Instantly the voice changed. Judy could tell that her fears were well founded.

"Yes, yes. About Irene. She's still missing. Who are her relatives in Brooklyn?"

"Why, I—I dunno," the old man faltered.

"You don't know! But you said not to worry. She was with relatives . . ."

"Didn't I say as she might be?"

"Then you *didn't* know where she was?" Judy demanded.

"N-no, not for sure. She'd have a purty hard time findin' abody from jest the looks of their house. But she does have relatives—if they ain't dead."

"Her mother's relatives?"

"Yes, my poor Annie's folks. I told her about them in a letter, but I get all muddled up on the names. Can't seem to remember. It's queer how anything like that slips a man's mind. Can't you help me, Judy?" he begged. "Ain't there anything you can do?"

"There's *every*thing. Why, we would have turned New York inside out looking for her if it hadn't been for that telegram——"

Dale touched her arm. "Go easy, Judy. Her father's upset, too. Better hang up, and we'll report it to the police again."

At the same time Mr. Lang was saying, "I'll manage it somehow. The nurses ain't strong enough to keep me here when my little girl is lost."

Through tear-dimmed eyes, Judy fumbled for the pile of coins, put the few that were left back in her pocketbook and stumbled out of the store with Dale and Pauline.

"All this to go through again," she moaned, "and after we believed she was safe!"

Then she looked up and saw Dale's sober face and resolved to be brave herself.

"We're going to the police station, aren't we?" she asked. "We'll tell them it was a mis-

take—that report that she was with relatives
—and perhaps, if we hurry, there will still be
time for a police broadcast of Irene's description over the radio tonight!''

"There must be time," Dale said between set
lips. "And then what?"

"And then," Judy declared, "we're going to
take paper and pencil and write down every
possible thing that could have happened to
Irene. After that we're going to begin with the
most plausible and follow up every clue. We'll
call in the police where necessary but we are
the ones to do the brain work. We are the ones
who care.''

# CHAPTER XVI

## OVER THE RADIO

LIEUTENANT COLLINS was a big man with a ruddy face and blue eyes that smiled kindly over his massive desk. Like Chief Kelly at home he inspired confidence, and Judy felt relieved to be talking with him instead of the young sergeant they had found at the police station before. With now and then an additional bit of information from Dale and Pauline, she retold the story of Irene's mysterious disappearance. Then she explained Mr. Lang's subsequent telegram leading them to suppose Irene was safe and, finally, the discovery that Mr. Lang had merely described a house in Brooklyn.

"You see, he lives in a small town. He didn't realize that such a description would be of no use to Irene here. And now," Judy finished, "we seem to be right back where we started from—without a clue."

By this time quite a group of officers and young detectives had gathered around the lieutenant's desk.

"It's beginning to look like an interesting case," one of them remarked with a smug satisfaction that caused Dale to glare at him. Irene was no case! She was a flesh-and-blood girl—lost, alone. He did not think of the many instances in his own stories where the detective had made similar remarks. It never occurred to him that here was real experience on which to build his imaginative tales. No one had told him that the one thing his stories lacked was an intensity of feeling gained only by living through an actual tragedy.

Judy thought of it. It seemed irrelevant, almost disloyal to Irene to think of fiction and Dale's future just then. But if they found Irene, Dale's future might be hers. How wonderful! And after those high-hat girls in Farringdon had snubbed her so! It would be almost a triumph for Judy, too—that is, if they could only find Irene and give this Cinderella story a chance to come true.

The printed form Judy had previously filled in was still on file in the police records. This was checked up and once more turned over to the Detective Bureau. The description, Lieutenant Collins promised, would be telephoned to the Bureau of Missing Persons and broadcast over the radio at seven-thirty.

Dale looked at his watch. Only an hour and the whole country would be hearing about Irene's disappearance. Surely someone had seen her, and whoever it was couldn't forget the golden dress and slippers.

"Girls don't vanish," Judy declared as they turned to leave.

"Oh, but they do," Pauline cried. "Joy Holiday vanished right out of a locked room. And when they found her she was dead."

None of them spoke after that. Automatically they went back to the house and climbed up the three long flights of stairs. Blackberry greeted them as they opened the door, but Judy had no heart for romping with him.

"Go away!" she said, pushing him gently out of the way. "Cats can't understand human troubles."

But instead of minding her, he rubbed his silky head against her ankles. His soft, crackly purr seemed to say: "Cats do understand human troubles. What you need is someone who loves you to sympathize.''

Tears came to Judy's eyes. She thought of her father and mother struggling with an epidemic of influenza when they had wanted a vacation. She thought of her brother, Horace. She thought of Peter and Honey and their two dear grandparents, of Arthur who had once helped hunt for Lorraine Lee in his airplane. How she missed them all! How she needed them! Oh, why had she and Irene ever left Farringdon at all? To find adventure, she supposed. Now she felt sick to death of adventure and only wanted all her friends together the way they used to be. Irene, even the pale overworked Irene, would be better than this awful uncertainty.

Walking over to the radio, Judy stood watching Dale as he fumbled with the dials. In ten more minutes the police alarms would be on the air.

"A little more to the left if you want the city station," Pauline directed from her chair beside the desk. He turned the dials and, loud and clear, a familiar dance tune broke upon their senses.  It was *Golden Girl* and a well-known radio artist, Kate South, was singing in an emotional, contralto voice:

My own golden girl.  There is one, only one
Who has eyes like the stars and hair like the
  sun.
In your new yellow gown you're a dream of
  delight.
You have danced in my heart on bright
  slippers tonight . . .

Judy bowed her head and tears smarted in her eyes.

"Irene's description," Dale said fiercely. He shut off the radio and did not turn it on again until the ten minutes were up.

Gongs sounded and then the announcer's voice, very cold and matter-of-fact, read through the list of missing persons.  Irene's name came last:

MISSING SINCE JUNE TWENTIETH: IRENE LANG OF FARRINGDON, PENNSYLVANIA; VISITING AT 120 GRAMERCY PARK, NEW YORK CITY.  SEVENTEEN YEARS OLD; HEIGHT: 5 FEET, 4 INCHES; WEIGHT: 110 POUNDS; BLUE EYES; FAIR HAIR; WEARING A YELLOW DRESS AND JACKET, NO HAT, HIGH HEELED GOLD PUMPS AND CARRYING A BROWN HAND BAG.

That was all. In a few seconds it was over and Judy was left with the sick feeling that no one had heard.

In the living room of their little apartment two hundred miles away, Mrs. Dobbs settled herself in a comfortable rocker ready to relax and listen to the radio. Mrs. Dobbs loved music. Usually she listened to the old-time melodies but there was something especially appealing about the popular song that Kate South was singing. She called to her grandson.

"Come here, Peter, and listen."

The tall youth entered the room and stretched himself in a chair.

"Gee, Grandma! It makes a fellow feel lonesome. Why the dickens do you suppose Judy had to spend her vacation so far away from folks who care about her?"

"She's with Irene," Mrs. Dobbs replied, "and from what I hear, Pauline Faulkner has taken a great liking to both of them. Honey was saying only this morning that she wished she'd been invited, too."

"I'm glad she wasn't," Peter returned with

vigor. "At least I have a little to say about what my sister is and isn't going to do. Where is she now?"

"Out with Horace. He's been taking her out alone since Irene went away——"

But Mrs. Dobbs stopped speaking as Peter held up his hand. The music had played out and neither of them had been paying much attention to the announcements that followed until the name, Irene Lang, broke upon their senses. Missing, was she?

Peter gave a low whistle of surprise and then jumped to his feet.

"Where are you going?" his grandmother cried.

"Going to get the car," he flung over his shoulder. "Judy will be needing me."

In the hallway he bumped into Horace and Honey just returning from a short walk through town.

"Where's the fire?" Horace greeted him. "If there's something exciting going on I want to hear about it. The paper's starving for news."

"Irene Lang has disappeared!" Peter gave

out the "news" so suddenly that Horace was dumbfounded for a moment.

"And I'm going to New York to help Judy," he added. "She's apt to go too far with her flare for detecting. You might as well come, too. Maybe the paper will finance the trip if we bring back a big scoop——"

"Sa-ay!" Horace broke in. "Don't forget it's Irene Lang who is missing. News or no news, nothing goes into the paper that isn't on the level."

"Don't I know it!" Peter replied. "Irene wouldn't do anything that wasn't on the level and there's Judy to consider, too."

"I want to help," Honey spoke up. "Won't you let me come with you?"

Horace looked at her and shook his head. The trip wouldn't be a very safe one with Peter in his present mood and his car capable of a speed exceeding sixty.

"Then can't we do something here?" she begged. "Can't we go and see Irene's father? Maybe he knows where she went."

"Gosh!" Horace exclaimed. "That's a real idea, Honey. You'll be as good as Judy if you keep on using those little gray cells of yours.

Goodbye, Peter! We're off for the sanitarium.''

"Backing out, eh?'' Peter gibed him.

"Backing out, nothing! If we learn anything important,'' Horace declared, "we can beat your car in Arthur's airplane.''

## CHAPTER XVII

### THE ONLY ANSWER

AND yet Judy felt that no one had heard, that it was all up to her. Even Dale Meredith seemed not to be helping, and Pauline . . . How much did Pauline care? Neither of them had attempted to follow Judy's suggestion that they write down every possible clue. Instead they talked—talked until midnight, almost—when she was trying so hard to think.

Then Mary came in. Mary usually came in when Pauline stayed up too late. The cocoa that she served was a signal for Dale to leave and the girls to retire.

Pauline drank her cocoa quickly and walked with him to the door. When it closed behind him she still stood there, her head pressed against the panels.

"You're tired," Judy told her. "I'll take this cocoa into my room and let you sleep."

"Aren't you going to drink it?"

Judy shook her head. "Not with Irene gone. It would make me sleepy too, and I've simply got to think."

Alone in her room she tried to turn herself into an abstract thing, a mental machine that could think without feeling. In her heart she could not believe Irene had taken the poetry, but in her mind she knew that it must be so.

Didn't Irene want the poems because they described a house? Even the address might have been among the conglomeration of papers. When her father suggested that she visit relatives in Brooklyn he had described a house also. Perhaps the two descriptions were the same! Perhaps the relative she sought was Sarah Glenn! For surely it was more than coincidence that Irene looked so much like the poet's daughter, Joy Holiday. Could she have been an aunt? No, because Sarah Glenn had only the one child. A distant cousin? Hardly. Then there was only one conclusion left: Joy Holiday might have been Irene's own mother!

Could Irene have put two and two together, just as Judy was doing, and gone to the poet's house the day she disappeared? No doubt, if she did, she planned to be back again before either Judy or Pauline returned. Something had prevented her!

That something might have been Jasper Crosby, cruel, scheming, mercenary creature that he was. Or it might have been poor, demented Sarah Glenn. She might have locked Irene in the tower the way she had once locked her own daughter away from her friends. There was no telling what a crazy woman might do!

An hour later Judy still sat on her bed, trying to decide what to do. Her cocoa, on a forgotten corner of the dresser, had crusted over like cold paste. She rose, walked across the room, tasted the cold drink and set down the cup. She must come to some decision! Irene might be living through a nightmare of torture in that horrible house Sarah Glenn had described in her poems.

In the next room Pauline was sleeping soundly. Judy could wake her, ask her advice. Downstairs the telephone waited ready to help her. She could call Lieutenant Collins at the police station and tell her findings to him. She could telephone Mr. Lang again and ask him more questions—worry him more. She could call the young author, Dale Meredith.

Yes, she could call Dale and tell him that the insane poet might be Irene's grandmother; that the scheming miser, Jasper Crosby, might be her uncle and that Irene, herself, had probably stolen the poetry to help locate them. What a shock that would be to the young author who had idolized Irene and called her his Golden Girl. Judy hadn't the heart to disillusion him although her own spirit was heavy with the hurt of it all.

She wouldn't notify the police either. Irene must not be subjected to an unkind cross fire of questions when, or if, she did return. Judy would find Irene herself and let her explain. Suppose she had stolen the poetry? What did it matter? Judy was learning not to expect perfection in people. She would love Irene all the more, forgiving her. And if Irene had stolen the poetry she could give it back quietly, and Judy could explain things to Emily Grimshaw. Dale need never be told.

Judy wouldn't have done that much to shield herself. She could . . . Oh, now she knew she could stand shock, excitement, tragedy. But it wouldn't do to have people blaming Irene.

That night Judy buried her head in the pillows waiting, wide-eyed, for morning. Morning would tell. She knew that work was slack at the office and that Emily Grimshaw often did not come in until afternoon. She would take the morning off and go . . . she consulted the bit of paper with the poet's latest verse on one side and her address scribbled on the other. She got up out of bed to take it from her pocketbook and study it. The street apparently had no name.

*One blk. past Parkville, just off Gravesend Avenue.*

## CHAPTER XVIII

### IN THE TOWER WINDOW

MORNING dawned cold and misty. Judy fumbled through the closet hunting for an umbrella, and her trembling fingers touched Irene's clothes. They lingered lovingly in the folds of each well remembered dress.

"Irene! Irene!" she thought. "I don't care what you've done if only I can bring you back."

In the adjoining room Pauline was still asleep. How cruel of her to sleep! No one was up except Blackberry, out there on the roof garden. Feeling that she must say goodbye to somebody, Judy whispered it to him.

It was too early for the throng of office workers to be abroad when Judy stepped out on the wet pavement and turned toward the subway entrance. The tall buildings in lower New York were little more than shadows, and the clock in the Metropolitan Tower was veiled in mist. Ghostly halos were around all the street lamps, and dampness seemed to have settled heavily over everything.

Judy felt it. The only comforting thing about the trip was the fact that she would be riding on the subway alone for the first time. She paid her fare, asked a few directions, and soon was seated in an express train bound for Brooklyn.

She pressed her forehead against the window as the train came onto Manhattan Bridge and started its trip over the East River. Freighters steamed down toward the ocean and up again. Everything looked gray.

As she watched, Judy's hopes sank lower and lower. She began to realize that it was not the part of wisdom to go on her dangerous errand to the poet's house alone. What would she say if Jasper Crosby opened the door? Would her experience with eccentric Emily Grimshaw help her to cope with the insane hallucinations of Sarah Glenn? Would she dare demand to know what had happened to Irene when a possibility existed that they had never seen her? Suppose they asked for the missing poetry. If she lied to defend Irene her nervousness might betray her. Judy knew that her chances of

finding her chum were slim, very slim.  Like
the shining tracks behind her they seemed to
lessen as the train sped on.

At Ninth Avenue she changed to the Culver
Line.  Up came the train, out of the tunnel, and
the wet gray walls at the side of the tracks grew
lower and lower.  Soon they were clear of the
ground and Judy realized that this was the
elevated.  Only four more stations!  She looked
around, eager for her first glimpse of Brooklyn,
but what she saw caused her to shudder.

"Ugh!  A graveyard."

It stretched on and on, a grim sight on that
dreary morning.  Even after the white stones
were left behind vacant lots and empty buildings made the scene look almost as cheerless.

At the fourth stop Judy got off and went
down to the street.  It was silly, but the thought
came to her that if ever spirits walked abroad
they would walk along Gravesend Avenue.

Consulting the slip of paper, she counted
blocks as she passed them and watched for
Parkville Avenue.  She knew the old-fashioned
street at once from the quaint houses that lined
it.  Then came the Long Island Railroad cut
with a long line of box cars passing under

Gravesend Avenue in a slow-moving procession.

She paused. Could the alley beyond be the street she sought? No wonder they hadn't named it anything. Why, it wasn't even paved! It seemed little more than a trail through vacant lots. She hesitated, looked ahead and caught her breath in a quick, terrified gasp. Then she stared, open-mouthed. There was something sinister about the huge, gray frame building that loomed in her path. The gnarled old trees surrounding it seemed almost alive, and the wind whistling through their branches sounded like a warning. But it was the tower, not the house itself, that caused Judy to gasp. The whole lower part of it was burned away and in the tower window something thin and yellow moved back and forth behind the curtains. It looked like an elongated ghost!

Judy rubbed her eyes and looked again. This time the tower was dark with the even blackness of drawn shades behind closed windows.

An unreasonable fear took possession of the watching girl. She felt that she had seen something not there in material substance. Stanza after stanza of Sarah Glenn's poetry forced itself upon her consciousness, and it all fitted this house—the yellow ghost in the window, the crumbling tower.

Suddenly Judy realized that she was standing stock-still in the middle of the muddy unpaved street, moving her lips and making no sound. She was doing the same thing that Emily Grimshaw had done when Dale Meredith said she was crazy. Oh! She must get control of herself, take herself in hand.

"If the house can frighten me like this," she thought, "what wouldn't it do to Irene?"

Bracing her slim shoulders and mustering all her courage, Judy marched up on the porch and felt for the bell. Finding none, she rapped with her bare knuckles. The sound of her rap sent an echo reverberating through the walls of the still house.

Judy waited. She waited a long time before she dared rap again. The house seemed to be inhabited only by the echo she had heard and the phantom that had vanished from the tower window.

Still nobody answered. Judy tried the door and found it locked. Then she peered through the lower windows and saw at once that the house was empty of furniture.

"Nobody lives here," she told herself and then she told herself the same thing all over again so that it would surely seem true. "Nobody ever does live in empty houses."

And yet she had the strangest feeling that she was being watched!

# CHAPTER XIX

## LIKE A FAIRY TALE

HER nerves taxed to the breaking point, Judy gave up searching for the day and went to the office. Emily Grimshaw was not there but she had left a message:

*Will be away for a time and leave you in charge.*

"Me in charge!" Judy exclaimed. She couldn't imagine herself conducting Emily Grimshaw's business sensibly. "I'll just close up for the day," she decided in exasperation. Leaving a notice to that effect at the hotel desk, she locked the office and started for Dr. Faulkner's house.

In the entrance hall she was met by an anxious group of faces. Dale's, Pauline's—and Peter's.

"Judy!" he cried, and then when her only answer was a choked sob, again, "Judy!"

"Oh, Peter! You'll help?"

"That's why I'm here. We telephoned

127

*every*where.  We thought you'd never come.''

"Where on earth were you?" Dale asked.

"Hunting for Irene," Judy explained brokenly. "I—I followed up a clue.  I thought I knew where Irene was and I went out there to get her to—to bring her home and surprise you, but she wasn't there."

"Wasn't *where?*"

"Where I thought she was . . . the most awful place just off Gravesend Avenue out in old Parkville.  The—the house has a tower, just like the tower in Sarah Glenn's poems.  It's burned halfway up and—and—and——"

"And what, Judy?  Don't act so frightened."

"There was something in the tower," she blurted out, "something yellow——"

"Probably a yellow dog or some such ordinary thing," Pauline interrupted.

"Oh, but it wasn't!  I saw it as plainly as anything, and it looked like a woman in a yellow robe, only she was too tall and too thin to be real.  Then I looked again and she was gone but I could still feel her watching me.  It was awful!  I didn't think there could be a tower of flame or a ghost, but there they were!" Judy leaned back against the closed door and threw both hands outward in a gesture of bewilderment.

"And I always thought I was a practical person. I always trusted my own head—and eyes."

Impulsively, Peter caught her hands in his. His voice was husky. "I still trust them, Judy. Tell me everything," he pleaded. "I know you must have had a good reason for thinking that Irene might be in this queer old house. Why did you?"

"Because Irene looks so much like the poet's daughter, Joy Holiday. I thought they might be related. Mr. Lang spoke of Irene's relatives. He told her to look them up. But the poet is crazy! Anything might happen!"

"And yet you went there alone!" Peter exclaimed. "Don't you realize that whatever happened to Irene might have happened to you?"

"I did realize it—when I got there," Judy faltered. "I—I guess I wasn't very brave to run away, but nobody seemed to live in the house. It looked—empty."

"Then, of course, Irene couldn't be there," Pauline concluded.

"Oh, but they might have moved—*and taken*

*her with them!''* Judy turned to Peter, a new
fear in her eyes. ''You know about law. Tell
me, if Irene is related to Sarah Glenn wouldn't
she inherit some of her property?''

''That depends upon the will,'' he replied.
''If she made a will before she went insane——''

''She did!'' Judy interrupted. ''She willed
the property to her daughter and, in the event
of her death, it was to go to her brother, Jasper Crosby. He's a crook and a scoundrel,''
she declared, ''worse than Slippery McQuirk or
any of Vine Thompson's gang, if I'm any judge
of character. You see, if Irene is related to the
poet through Joy Holiday, how convenient it
would be for him to have her out of the way?''

''You mean that Joy Holiday might have
been Irene's mother?''

''She couldn't have been,'' Pauline spoke up.
''Joy Holiday has been dead for twenty years.''

''Supposedly! Her mother never did believe
the body was hers, and even Emily Grimshaw
says it didn't look like her.''

''Where'd they get the body?'' Peter asked.

''Jasper Crosby went to the morgue and got
it. He identified it as Joy's, and people paid

no attention to his sister's objections because they knew she was insane."

"Then this girl, Joy Holiday, is legally dead. But if we can prove that there has been a fraud . . ."

"What fraud?" Dale questioned. "You don't mean to tell us that this Jasper Crosby may have falsely identified some unknown girl's body in order to inherit his sister's property?"

"That's exactly what I was trying to say. I don't know anything about Irene's mother and neither does she. Mr. Lang only remembered the name, Annie, and that, as well as Joy, may have been only a nickname." Judy turned to Peter. "I know how you felt when your parents were a mystery. Well, wouldn't Irene feel the same way? Her father gave away some family history in his letter, and Irene was more impressed than we know by Emily Grimshaw's collapse. Remember, I wrote you about it, Peter? She wanted to find out about her mother——"

"Then she did take the poetry," Pauline put in.

"Yes," Judy agreed. "I'm afraid she did. It's a terrible thing not to know the truth about one's parents, and Irene must have taken the poetry to help her find that horrible house that seems to have swallowed her up."

"She said she didn't," Dale maintained.

Judy felt suddenly ashamed that his trust in Irene should be greater than hers. But if, distrusting her, Judy found her, then she could be glad of her disbelief.

"There is another possibility," she ventured and made her voice sound more hopeful than she felt. "There is the possibility that Irene may be safe in the poet's house."

"That sounds more plausible," Dale agreed, "but you said the house was empty."

"I said it *looked* empty, except for that unearthly thing in the tower. But, now that I think of it, something alive must have been there to pull the shades. Do you suppose," Judy asked in a tremulous whisper, "that somebody could be locked there like Joy Holiday was when she vanished?"

"It sounds like a fairy tale, doesn't it? But not," Peter added gravely, "if Irene is in the tower. Judy, we must do something—and do it quickly."

It did not take him long to decide what that

something would be. "We'll get a policeman to go with us," he declared. "The police have a right to force their way into a house if nobody answers."

"Without a search warrant?" questioned Pauline.

"That's the dickens of it," Dale fumed. "There's sure to be some red tape attached to it and loss of time may mean—loss of Irene. We've got to convince the police that this is a matter of life and death!"

A taxi was the quickest means of getting to the police station. It took considerable explaining, however, to convince officials that the case was urgent. The fact that the owner of the house was known to be insane and that Irene might be held there against her will proved to be the strongest argument in favor of the search warrant they requested. But it could not be served until the following day.

"You have to go before a magistrate," Lieutenant Collins explained, "and night warrants are allowed only in cases where persons or property are positively known to be in the place to be searched. However, there are several ways of getting around that. If a felony has been committed, as in the present case, we don't need a warrant.''

"What felony?" Judy asked.

"Great guns!" he exclaimed. "Don't you call kidnaping a felony? If the girl's held there against her will it's a plain case of kidnaping!''

Judy hadn't thought of that. Kidnapers and killers were almost synonymous in her mind and the thought was terrifying.

Lieutenant Collins wasted no further time but called the Parkville Precinct, and two policemen were detailed to meet Judy, Pauline, Dale and Peter and accompany them to the house with the crumbling tower.

# CHAPTER XX

NEITHER Peter nor Dale stopped to count the cost of taxicabs that night. The driver hesitated only a moment. Their request that he make the fastest possible time to the distant Brooklyn police station was not a usual one. Knowing that it must be urgent, the driver made good his promise and soon they were speeding across Manhattan Bridge, through side streets in reckless haste and then down the long stretch of boulevard. Judy leaned out of the window and searched the scene ahead for a trace of anything familiar.

Ocean Parkway, lined with its modern dwelling houses and new apartment buildings was as unlike Gravesend Avenue as anything could be. Still, the two were only a few blocks apart. The driver turned his cab down a side street, sure of his bearings; and Judy, watching, saw the sudden change. The boulevard with its lights and stream of traffic, then queer old

Parkville, a village forgotten while Brooklyn grew up around it.

The police station looked all the more imposing in this setting. Two young policemen were already there, waiting beside the high desk and talking with the captain.

Sarah Glenn's house was only a short distance away, and together they walked it. Soon they were turning down the unpaved end of the street that bordered the railroad cut.

"There it is!" Judy shivered a little and drew her coat closer as she pointed.

The house was dark and silent. The windows were black—black with an unfathomable blackness that must be within. Peter sensed Judy's fear for he took her arm and guided her as they came up the broken walk.

On the steps Dale stopped and picked up a white flower.

"What can it mean?" Pauline whispered. "How would a rose get here?"

He shook his head. "It's beyond me. What's this?" He fingered a lavender ribbon that was still attached to the door.

"Looks as if there'd been a funeral here," one of the police officers observed.

Both girls stood trembling as he banged and pounded on the door and then shouted a threat to the still house.

"Nobody home," he turned and said. "Do you think it's necessary to force our way in?"

"More than ever," Judy replied. "We *must* see what's in the tower!"

"Okay! Give me a hand, partner, and we'll smash the door."

Underneath the porch they found a beam which would serve their purpose. Peter and Dale helped the policemen, and soon the heavy door gave way and crashed into the empty house. A sickening, musty smell combined with the heady odor of flowers greeted them as they stepped inside.

"A funeral all right!" the policeman re-iterated. "Get the perfume, don't you? But everything's cleared up—except . . ." He and Judy had seen it at the same time but the policeman was the first to pick it up. ". . . this card."

"Let me see it."

Obligingly he handed it to the girl. She turned it over in her hand and passed it on to Dale. It read:

*With deepest sympathy*
*Emily Grimshaw*

"Do you know the party?" the other officer asked.

"My employer," Judy replied simply.

The question in her mind, however, was less easily answered. Was Emily Grimshaw's absence from her office explainable by this death? Whose death? If Emily Grimshaw had sent flowers certainly she must know.

The policemen were busy searching the house, and Judy and her three companions followed them. The rooms upstairs, like those on the first floor, were empty of furniture. But the tower room was found to open from a third floor bedroom. To their surprise, this room was completely furnished, even to bed coverings and pillows. A little kitchen adjoined it and there were evidences that food had recently been cooked there. An extra cot was made up in the hall.

So the poet and her brother had lived in their immense house and occupied only two rooms! Or three? They had yet to explore the tower. Peter Dobbs tried the door and found it locked.

"We'll have to break this one, too," the

policemen said, and Dale offered to get the beam.

Pauline's hand kept him. "Wait a minute," she pleaded. "It's a shame to spoil the door and maybe this key will fit."

She took a queer brass key from her hand bag. Judy and Peter frankly stared. The policemen, though obviously doubting its usefulness, consented to try it. To their astonishment, it turned.

"Where did you find that key?" Dale questioned.

"In the pocket of Irene's brown suit. I put it in my own hand bag for safe-keeping."

"Rather suspected it fitted something, didn't you?" he said sarcastically. "Well, to me it doesn't prove a thing."

"It does to me," Judy put in, "although not what you think. This must have been Joy Holiday's room when she was a child! And if Irene had the key surely Joy Holiday is related to her—perhaps her own mother!"

"It sounds like pretty sound figuring to me," Peter agreed, flashing a look of boyish admiration in Judy's direction.

Then, as the door swung open, they followed

the policemen into the tower. Peter pushed a
button and the light revealed a circular room
with a gay panorama of nursery rhyme characters frolicking across the wall.

Upon closer inspection, however, the room
was seen to be six-sided with shelves built into
two of its corners. On one of these dolls and
expensive toys were neatly arranged. Books
and games for a somewhat older girl adorned
the other shelf.

A curtained wardrobe concealed another corner, while a white cot bed, all freshly made, occupied the corner at the left of the door. The
two remaining corners were cleverly camou-
flaged by concave mirrors with uneven distort-
ing surfaces, such as are sometimes seen in
amusement park funny houses. In spite of
Judy's anxiety, she could not suppress a smile
when the two policemen walked by them.

So this was the room where the poet had
locked Joy Holiday! Did she think those silly
mirrors and a roomful of books and toys could
make up for a lack of freedom? Judy, who
had always been allowed to choose what friends
she liked, could easily see why the poet's daughter had wanted to run away—or vanish as peo-

ple said she had done.  How strange it all was and how thrilling to be standing in the very room where Irene's mother had stood twenty years before!

"It's so quiet and peaceful here," Judy said. "Nothing very terrible could have happened in this pretty room."

She had momentarily forgotten that the whole lower structure of it had been burned away, that she had seen a tall yellow specter peering out of its window.

Peter, however, remembered the fantastic story Judy had told him.  It did not surprise the young law student that no one was in the tower.  He and the two policemen immediately set about looking for clues to Irene's whereabouts.  But it was not until Dale drew back the wardrobe curtain and they found her yellow dress and jacket hanging there that they became truly alarmed.  Now they knew, past any doubt, that Irene had visited her grandmother's house.  There had been a funeral!  Even if it had been Sarah Glenn's, Irene might have been with her when she died.  Alone with a crazy woman . . . timid little Irene!

It was a sober moment for all of them.

"That girl's been held captive all right," one of the policemen said in a voice more troubled than one would expect of an officer of the law. "It looks as if we've found the evidence right here."

He stood examining the folds of her yellow dress. It appeared to have been hanging in the wardrobe for some time. Other clothes were there, too, but the full skirts and puffed sleeves were in the style of twenty years ago. On a shelf above them were two or three queer little hats, all decked out with feathers and flowers. Irene would have laughed at them. She would have tried them on and posed before the comical mirrors. Judy wondered if she had done that.

Someone, apparently, had tried on one of the aprons. It was a simple gingham affair such as girls used to wear to protect dainty dresses, and it had been thrown carelessly over a chair. When Judy made a move to hang it up she was warned to leave everything exactly as it was.

"If this turns out to be a murder case," one of the policemen said, "this bedroom may contain important evidence." He turned to Dale who still held the rose he had found on the steps. "That flower proves that the funeral must have been held today. It's still sweet," he continued, making a grimace as he sniffed it. "We'll get together all the facts on the case and have the place watched. If this man, Jasper Crosby, returns tonight there'll be a policeman here to nab him. A general alarm will be dispatched to our radio cars, and we'll find out whose funeral it was, too, and let you know first thing in the morning."

"Oh, if you only would," Judy cried gratefully. "Perhaps you can find out from my employer. She's decided to take a vacation for some unknown reason but you may be able to locate her here."

She gave them Emily Grimshaw's home address. Peter Dobbs, who had taken a keen interest in the legal aspect of the case, jotted it down, too. Much to Dale's discomfiture, he kept talking about Irene.

"If we find her," he declared, "this may be my big opportunity. She would contest the will, of course, and I might be able to help her then."

"*If* we find her," Dale repeated doubtfully.

Later Peter gave Judy the address and telephone number of the hotel where he was staying. He would be either there or at the police station in case she needed him.

"If I do call you," Judy promised, with an attempt at lightness, "you may be sure that I'm in trouble because it's really your place to call me."

# CHAPTER XXI

### ANOTHER JULIET

No MATTER what happens the trivialities of life must go on. Food must be cooked and eaten, no matter how dry it tastes. Work must be done. Judy knew that and dragged her tired body out of bed. She dressed and went down into the kitchen where Mary made coffee and brought out the toaster. Pauline had left for school, she said. Would Judy mind the toast herself?

She nodded, staring at the coffeepot and wondering if Irene would ever sit across the breakfast table and drink coffee with her again. She let the toast burn and threw it away. Then she put on a second piece, watched it until it turned golden brown and flipped it over.

The doorbell rang!

Always, when the doorbell rang, there came that sudden exaltation. It might be news of Irene! Peter might have found her! With each new disappointment Judy's hopes for Irene's safe return sank lower.

This time it was not Peter. It was Arthur Farringdon-Pett, the young pilot-engineer, who owned his own airplane and had taken Judy for a never-to-be-forgotten ride far above the beautiful St. Lawrence River. Judy's brother, Horace, stood in the doorway beside him, and both of them looked as if they had not slept for a week. Horace's usually sleek hair was disordered and Arthur needed a shave. He was the first to speak.

"Any news of Irene?"

"Didn't you bring any?" she asked. And before they could answer she went on saying how sure she was that they must have news or they wouldn't have flown all the way to New York. She could tell they had been flying as they were still dressed for it.

"We were in too much of a hurry to bother changing these togs at the hangar where I left the plane," Arthur explained.

"That's all right," Judy murmured, trying to shake off the queer feeling she had that he was some stranger.

"We do have news," Horace told her finally,

"but, I'm sorry to say, it's not news of Irene."

"What is it then?"

"News of her mother. We thought it might help you find her. I mean Irene. Her mother, of course, is dead."

"I knew that," Judy said. "But she has relatives. I'm sure your news will help me." Taking their things, she invited the boys to sit down and share her breakfast while they told her. She poured out the extra coffee Mary had made and pushed her brother into a chair. Arthur found his own and soon all three were seated beside the table. The boys explained their delay.

They had expected to arrive a day earlier but when Horace and Honey called at the sanitarium they found that Mr. Lang was gone. Immediately, Horace telephoned Arthur who agreed to help search for him in his plane. It would have been easy to find him if, as they expected, he had taken the straight road for New York. But his crippled legs gave out and, toward evening, they found him helpless in the edge of a deep wood. Here, while they were waiting for the ambulance to take him back to the hospital, Mr. Lang told his story.

When Tom Lang was a young man, only eighteen or twenty, he had worked as a chauffeur for a wealthy family in Brooklyn. The daughter of the house gave parties, a great many of them, and after the parties Tom would drive the whole crowd of young people home. He never paid much attention to them until, one night, a new girl came to a party. She was different from all the others. She had glamour, radiance, all the qualities a man wants in a girl. But the young chauffeur dared not hope that she would have any use for him. She only came to the one party—like a princess in her golden dress and slippers. He took her home and remembered the house. After that he would drive past it, always hoping that she would see him.

And one day she did! She waved to him from the tower window. Finally he understood, from the motion of her hand, that she wanted to come down—and couldn't. The door locked from the outside, and her tiny key was of no use from within. Clutching it in her hand, she leaned farther and farther out of the tower window.

Just like the princess in Tom's old fairy

book. He would be the brave knight and rescue
her. There was a rope in the car. It had been
used as a towing rope but would now serve a
nobler purpose.

He swung one end of it up to the tower; he
saw the slim white hand reach out and grasp
it, the lithe body throw itself over the window
sill and descend—slowly, slowly. She was almost to the ground when the rope came loose
from where she had fastened it.

She fell!

Quick as a flash, Tom Lang caught her in his
strong young arms. That same day he made
her his bride. She lived just long enough to
bear him a little daughter, the image of herself. Heartbroken, Irene's father had never
spoken of her. But he had saved her golden
wedding dress and on Irene's seventeenth
birthday sent it to her with a letter explaining
his gift and enclosing the key to her tower
room. His Annie had been just seventeen.

"Romantic, wasn't it?" Arthur asked after
Horace had told the story as only a reporter
could tell it.

Judy, who had listened to it all without making any comment, admitted that it was the **most** romantic true story she had ever heard.

"But Mr. Lang didn't give Irene the name or address," Arthur said thoughtfully. "He only sent the key to her mother's room because he wanted her to have it as a remembrance. In fact, he told so little in his letter that it seems impossible—unthinkable—that she could have found her grandmother——"

"Unless she found the same description somewhere else," Judy interrupted.

"Yes, but where?"

"In her grandmother's poems. She and I read them together."

Judy did not add that the manuscripts were now missing and that she felt almost certain that Irene had taken them to help locate her relatives. That knowledge was confined to four persons: Pauline, Dale Meredith, Peter and herself.

The fact that Irene's grandmother wrote poems surprised Arthur. He had heard the popular song, *Golden Girl,* but had never connected it with Irene, probably, because he had never seen her in her mother's golden dress.

"And you say the poet's name is Glenn?"

"It's really Holiday," Judy explained. "She wrote under a nom de plume."

But the boys couldn't remember ever hearing the name Joy Holiday. Mr. Lang had called his wife simply Annie.

When Judy had finished a complete account of the police search through Sarah Glenn's house they were more puzzled than ever. But they appeared to be simply puzzled—not alarmed.

"We'll find out all about it," Horace promised, "when we find Irene."

It was good to hear them saying "when." It gave Judy new courage. She would need courage to get through that day. She told them her plans. First they were to get in touch with the police to learn what they could of the funeral that had been held in Sarah Glenn's house. Judy then suggested that Horace and Arthur call on Dale Meredith and ask his advice while she spent a few hours in Emily Grimshaw's office.

"I'll be of more use there than anywhere else," she said. "Besides, it's my job and I'm being paid for it. Irene comes first, of course. But the police are doing all they can, and if I could see Emily Grimshaw and talk with her—well, I might find out some things that even the police don't know. We discovered a card on the floor when we searched the poet's house. It showed that my employer must have attended the funeral.''

Both boys agreed that Emily Grimshaw's office was the place for Judy. Knowing that there must be stacks of papers for her to read and correct, Judy even consented to their plan that she go to the office at once and await news of Irene there. They would go on to the Parkville police station and telephone her. Peter had gone there and they might meet him.

After giving them explicit directions, Judy walked with them as far as the subway station at Union Square. There they separated, Judy taking the uptown train while the boys boarded an express for Brooklyn.

Horace turned to Arthur and spoke above the roar of the train.

''What puzzles me is how Irene found that house with nothing but a few crazy verses to go by, and I think that Judy knows if only she would tell.''

"She certainly knows something more," he agreed, "but I'm not worrying.  Judy is on the square."

"I believe she is," Horace replied, "but what about Irene?"

## CHAPTER XXII

### TRAPPED

Just as she had expected, Judy found plenty
of work waiting for her. The clerk at the hotel
desk gave her a pile of manuscripts left by
hopeful young authors. She glanced through
these, waiting for the telephone to ring. All of
them seemed inexcusably bad. Why, she wondered, did so many people waste their time trying to write when they had no idea of plot
construction or character development? . . .
Why didn't the telephone ring? Peter must
have had time to reach the police station.

One of Emily Grimshaw's old clients came in
and offered Judy another book manuscript.
This was better than the others. She promised
to read it.

"But where is Miss Grimshaw?" the author
asked.

"Away," Judy said briefly. "She left me
in charge."

Cautioning her to take care of the manuscript, the caller left. Judy's despondent mood returned. It all seemed such a futile undertaking, helping struggling young authors who were trying to write about life when life itself was so much more important—Irene's life.

At last the telephone rang and Judy recognized Arthur's voice.

"We just missed Peter. Did he call you?"

"Not yet," Judy answered.

"Then he couldn't have heard the latest police report! The man who lets garage space to Jasper Crosby saw him driving out of the garage yesterday, and a girl was with him. It might have been Irene? That was in the morning, an hour or so after you called at the house. We haven't learned anything else."

"Nothing about the funeral?"

"We haven't learned anything else," Arthur repeated. "Jasper Crosby's car is still out of the garage but the police have the license number. They'll be watching for him."

"Do you think he took Irene—away?" Judy's voice broke. She knew what might have happened and so did he. It was impossible to talk.

Dale Meredith called up a little later and

seemed very hopeful when he learned that Irene had been seen only the day before.

"She's alive then!" he cried.

"You mean she *was* alive," Judy amended gravely. "She must have been in the tower, and I was too frightened to do anything then. Now it may be too late. Jasper Crosby took her away in the car, and there was a funeral since then."

"I don't think it was Irene's funeral. Honestly, I don't. So keep on hoping and call me as soon as anything new develops."

Judy promised him that she would and turned to see the door slowly opening.

There stood Jasper Crosby himself!

"Where's Emily Grimshaw?" he demanded.

It took courage of the highest order for Judy to answer him calmly, in a businesslike voice. But she knew that she must. He must not know that she had ever seen or heard of Irene. She must not reveal that she had ever been near the house with the crumbling tower.

Assuming the manner of a disinterested clerk, she replied, "Miss Grimshaw is away. She left me in charge. What can I do for you?"

"Plenty," he cried. An angry flush spread

over his face. "You can tell me for one thing what happened to my sister's poetry. The publishers say that they have never seen it."

Judy pretended surprise. She rose and stood beside the man, her back against the door.

"There must have been some mistake," she went on. "You can search Miss Grimshaw's desk yourself and see if the poems are there."

"Thanks! I will."

He made a dive for the desk and began turning over papers recklessly, his hawk eyes searching every one.

Judy, with her back still against the door, turned the key in the lock, slowly, cautiously, so that he would not hear. Now she had him imprisoned in the room. He could not escape. But neither could she! For a moment she felt completely at his mercy.

"The poems aren't here," he announced in a voice that boded no good for Judy.

Quickly, then, she planned her course of action. She breathed a silent prayer that she might not fail. Aloud she said, "I'll call Emily Grimshaw and ask her what happened to the manuscripts."

He muttered something about making it

snappy and Judy walked over to the telephone. She began dialing a number. But it was not Emily Grimshaw's number. It was the number Peter Dobbs had given her!

"Hello!" his voice sounded over the wire.

Judy glanced at Jasper Crosby who stood near the desk. He was watching her like a cat.

"Hello! Miss Grimshaw? This is Judy. Jasper Crosby is here."

"Who? What?" Peter sputtered.

"Jasper Crosby. He's here in the office. He wants to know what happened to the poetry. Will you come right over?"

There followed a moment of silence. Jasper's eyes seemed to be taking an X-ray picture of Judy's mind. She felt that he must know she had not been talking to her employer. Then Peter's voice, lowered and tense, "You bet your life I'll come right over. And I'll have the whole police force with me. Brave little Judy!"

She replaced the receiver and turned to Jasper Crosby.

"She'll be right over. Will you wait?"

"Wait nothing," he muttered. "Why should

I wait? Say, who was that you were talking to then?"

"Emily Grimshaw," Judy lied gallantly.

"Mighty queer. She's home sick and then you call her up and she promises to get right up and come. Funny sickness, I call it."

"Who said she's sick?"

"Well, she took a fainting spell at the funeral yesterday."

"Whose funeral?"

He detected the anxious note in her voice and became suspicious.

"Nobody's business whose funeral it was. Emily Grimshaw can tell you. She was there. I'll be back later to see about the poetry."

"You're not going!" Judy cried in alarm as he turned toward the door.

"Why not? There's nothing to keep me."

Judy's thoughts answered him in a whirl. "Oh, but there is, Mr. Crosby. There's a locked door to keep you, and if you find out that I locked it you will know that I set a trap for you, that I must have known about Irene's disappearance. You'll be furious! You may kill me before Peter and the police get here."

In reality she said, "Please, Mr. Crosby. Miss Grimshaw will be only a minute and I would like to see this misunderstanding about the poetry cleared up."

"You would, eh? Interested, aren't you? So damned interested that you go prowling around our house like a thief."

This startled Judy so much that she could only gasp.

"What'd you want of my sister?" he demanded.

"I wanted to tell her about the poetry," Judy answered quickly. "You see, it's—it's lost."

"The deuce it is! Then how's Emily Grimshaw going to help matters by coming over?"

"She may know where it is. She was, well —intoxicated when it disappeared."

Jasper Crosby gave a dry chuckle. "Eh! heh! She can't even stay sober at a funeral. I'll be going now. Got to see a lawyer and sue the old lady for the loss of my sister's manuscripts."

"Oh, no! Wait a minute! Miss Grimshaw may have them. In fact, I'm almost sure she has," Judy cried in a panic. Anything to stall him, keep him talking until help came.

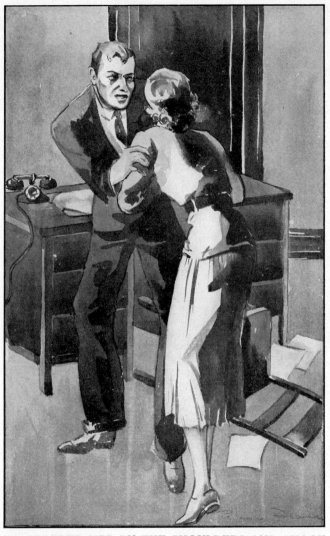

HE GRABBED HER BY THE SHOULDERS AND SHOOK
HER TILL SHE FELT DIZZY AND FAINT.

*The Yellow Phantom.*                                      *Page 161*

"Then tell her to send 'em to the publishers and make it snappy! I'm going."

Judy laid her hand firmly on his arm. "You're not going, Mr. Crosby. You're going to wait for Emily Grimshaw."

"Who's giving orders around here?" he snapped. "I tell you I'm going!"

Wrenching away from her, he bolted for the door.

Judy realized that she had held him off as long as she could. Now if Peter would only come—and come quickly!

Jasper Crosby tried the door. Then he turned to Judy with an oath. "So that's your game, is it? Well, it won't work. See? Better give me that key right now, sister."

"I will not give you the key."

"Then I'll take it from you!"

"You can't!" Judy cried as he lurched toward her. "You don't know where it is."

"Then you'll tell me!" He grabbed her by the shoulders and shook her until she felt dizzy and faint. "You'll tell me, do you hear?"

"I will—not," she gasped. "Let me go!"

His grip on her shoulders tightened. It hurt. It hurt terribly and Judy wanted to cry out for help.  But if she screamed the hotel clerk would force open the door and Jasper Crosby would be free.

"I'll tell you wh-where the key is," she managed to say.  "It's—it's in the small drawer of my desk under that pile of typewriter ribbon."

He looked at Judy shrewdly.  He knew better than that.  Judy was not used to deceiving people and her timidity betrayed her.

"You lie!" he shouted.  "That key's on you and I know it.  But I don't need a key.  I'll break down the door!"

"And rouse the whole hotel?" Judy asked quietly.

His hands clutched her throat now.  "Then give me the key!"

She could feel it, the cold little key that she had thrust down her neck.  It felt colder still when her breath was short.  She tried to scream but found she could make no sound.  It was then that she thought of his hands on Irene.  His relentless hands . . .

# CHAPTER XXIII

### TO THE RESCUE

"This way, officer. Here's the suite. Judy!" Peter Dobbs shouted.

One of the policemen rattled the door.

"It's locked," he announced, "and nobody answers. Give me your night stick, partner."

The sound of splintering wood announced that the door was open. The center panel, with Emily Grimshaw's unique knocker, fell to the floor and revealed the face of Jasper Crosby, white as a ghost. Judy lay limp at his feet.

"He's choked her!" Peter said between set teeth.

Before Jasper had time to turn his head he had him by the collar. One of the policemen clapped handcuffs over his wrists. The other two jerked him to a corner while Peter lifted Judy gently in his arms and placed her on the sofa.

"Brave little girl," he whispered and kissed her closed eyes.

She opened them, hardly believing that this was the same boy who had shared so many adventures with her. She had imagined Arthur kissing her—sometime when they grew older—but not Peter.

"I'm always needing someone to rescue me," she said, trying to laugh.

"And doesn't it make any difference who it is?" he asked.

"Yes, a little," she returned lightly. "I called you, didn't I?"

He studied her face, looking sorry about something, and after a few minutes he rose and said gruffly, "Come, we must hear what Jasper Crosby has to say for himself."

She followed him to the corner where the prisoner sat sullenly on a chair. At first he would say nothing, but later when Judy questioned him about the funeral his attitude changed.

"There's no secret about that," he declared. "My sister is the one who died. I'll give you the names of the doctor and undertaker to verify what I say."

"Then the funeral was Sarah Glenn's?"

Jasper nodded.

"But what became of Irene? We know she went to your sister's house and we know she never returned. Where is she?"

Jasper Crosby grinned. "I'll tell you if you're so anxious to know. I thought she was a mite young to be traveling about New York. Yes, Miss, a mite young and irresponsible. So I sent her back to her father. Even paid her train fare and saw her off. Pretty decent of me, don't you think, seeing she's a perfect stranger?"

"When did this happen?" Judy demanded.

Jasper Crosby let his eyes rove thoughtfully about the room before he answered. He seemed content that the girl, not the policemen, was questioning him. As Judy's questions were pertinent they, too, seemed content.

"I sent Irene to her father some time ago," he said finally.

"You were seen with her yesterday morning," said Judy.

"Ah, yes. Yesterday morning. That was it. I sent her home yesterday morning."

"Your two stories don't jibe," one of the policemen snapped.

"Yesterday morning is some time ago to

me," Jasper Crosby replied suavely. "Much has happened since then. There has been a funeral," he chuckled, "quite a funeral, too. Miss Grimshaw had a gay time of it all right, all right."

"Did Irene attend the funeral?" Judy asked, ignoring his last statement.

He looked surprised. "Oh, no indeed. She did not attend."

"You were pretty careful to keep her out of sight, weren't you?"

"She was with my sister constantly," he replied. "She had no desire to leave the house as long as my sister needed her."

Judy turned to Peter. "It doesn't sound true, does it?"

"It's the blackest lie I ever heard," he declared vehemently. "He can't tell us that Irene stayed with a crazy woman of her own free will and made no attempt to get in touch with her friends. There's been crooked work somewhere. If he sent Irene home, where is she now?" Peter questioned.

"Perhaps she's visiting someone else," Judy suggested hopefully.

Peter shook his head. "I don't believe it.

In any case she would have been in touch with you."

The policemen agreed that Jasper's story was not a very convincing one. Dale Meredith came in while they were still questioning him. Horace and Arthur were with him.

"I'll get something out of this bird," Horace declared. "Officer, have I your permission to question him?"

"Fire away," the policeman replied, "and more power to you!"

Horace turned to Jasper with flashing eyes.

"What did Irene say the day she came, and if, as you say, she is not your niece how did she happen to enter your sister's house?"

Jasper shrugged his shoulders and made a gesture indicating wheels going around.

"They cast spells, you know. Crazy people do. My sister's eyes took possession of Irene. Hypnotized her completely. I never saw two people so attached to each other. Crazy as loons, both of them."

"Irene Lang's mind was perfectly sound," Horace denied.

"I tell you my sister hypnotized her," Jasper maintained.

As Judy listened to the explanation that her brother drew from Jasper Crosby, she found herself almost believing it. Sarah Glenn's reaction to Irene's sudden appearance had been similar to Emily Grimshaw's, only more pronounced.

Jasper had been the one to open the door. Irene had inquired for her grandmother, but before he could speak the poet herself had rushed forward, almost smothering Irene in a tearful embrace.

"My Joy! My Joy! I *knew* you would come back."

Then she had turned to Jasper with accusing eyes. "I told you the child wasn't dead. Angels don't die. My darling! Darling!"

Again Irene had submitted to her embrace.

No amount of reasoning could dissuade the old lady from her queer conviction. She had seen her daughter's dead body, Jasper declared, but in spite of that she claimed this living girl as hers. Irene had answered to the name of Joy, pretended to remember touching little things out of the past, even fondled old playthings to please the poet. Like Golden Girl in the song she, too, had been a princess enthroned in her circular tower. There she had stayed. Jasper brought food, clothing, all the little things that a girl might need. He even moved a bed into the tower room so that she could sleep there. He called her Joy, too, to please his sister and pretended to think that she was the dead Joy Holiday returned.

"But the last few nights," he continued his narrative, "she caused some trouble. My sister died, very peacefully, with Irene at her bedside. But after that the girl refused to go to her room. She had an obsession that the tower wasn't safe and refused to sleep there."

"Well, is it safe?" Peter charged.

"It's been propped up ever since my sister tried to kill herself and set fire to the house. Sure, it's safe!"

"As long as the props hold."

Jasper Crosby gave a dry chuckle with no mirth in it. There was something maniacal about it—something that frightened Judy. She spoke to Peter in a low tone.

"He's trying to prove that Irene is insane just as he tried to prove, years ago, that her mother was dead. This time we won't let him get away with it."

"You bet we won't!" Peter, Arthur and Dale joined in agreement.

The policemen promised to make a check-up of train passengers to determine if any part of Jasper Crosby's story might be true.

"He's a mighty slippery prisoner," one of them said. "If he hadn't assaulted the girl there I doubt if we would be able to bring charges against him."

"Then I'm glad he did it," Judy said unexpectedly.

# CHAPTER XXIV

### PREMONITION

JUDY had a threefold reason for being glad.

She had accomplished Jasper Crosby's arrest, and except for a few bruises had suffered no ill effects from his frenzied choking.

In spite of doubts and suspicions as to the veracity of the prisoner's story, part of it must be true. Judy even dared hope that they were near the end of their search for Irene.

Also she was glad that Peter Dobbs had wanted to kiss her. It would be a new confidence to tell Irene when she came home.

All of them were saying "when" now. Arthur and Horace were busy mapping out plans for the day. They telephoned back to Farringdon to find out if anyone had seen Irene. The telephone calls were expensive and brought nothing but disappointment.

Even Pauline Faulkner seemed impressed when she heard of the terrifying things that had happened.

"And here I was in school, not helping at all, but today," she declared, "I'll make up for it. There isn't any more school until graduation and I'm free to help you. Emily Grimshaw's work has waited so long that there must be a deluge of unread manuscripts."

"It has waited so long that it can easily wait a little longer," Judy said.

"But isn't it important?"

"Not as important as finding Irene."

"I know, but haven't you done everything you can do? The boys can keep in touch with the police while I stay here and help you."

It really was best that way. And how kind of Pauline to offer to help! Dale suggested that she and Judy both go home and rest as soon as the work was done. But, unfortunately, it was Mary's day off.

"We'll bring in the dinner," Horace promised. "Any of you fellows know how to cook?"

Peter Dobbs volunteered.

"And just to make things even," Arthur put in, "I'll pay for it."

Judy laughed and felt better. She tackled the work with some of her old enthusiasm and succeeded in interesting Pauline in an unread manuscript.

After about an hour the telephone rang. It was Dale.

"Sorry," he said, "but it's beginning to look as if Jasper Crosby made up his story. No tickets to Farringdon have been purchased for a month."

"Are you at the police station?"

"Yes, and they've made a thorough check-up. The only answer is that Jasper Crosby lied. And he probably lied about Irene, too. I'd like to wring his neck!"

"So would I. But that's probably better left to the state. I only hope they make a good job of it. If they can prove that he lied it will make some difference in their treatment of him."

Undoubtedly it did make a difference as a detective called back later, and Judy found herself telling him even more than she had told Lieutenant Collins. The one thing she omitted was the fact that she believed Irene had stolen her grandmother's poetry. It was Jasper Crosby she was trying to have convicted, not Irene.

The case was being expertly handled. The

knowledge that Jasper Crosby was in jail, charged with assaulting Judy and kidnaping Irene, was some satisfaction. They would keep him right there, too, until Irene's whereabouts were known.

The day dragged on. Emily Grimshaw's work seemed to take longer now that Judy had lost heart again. It was good to have Pauline there helping. She read. She typed and when everything else was done she asked Judy if she might see her carbon copies of Sarah Glenn's poetry. "I wanted to read them myself," she said in explanation. "It's a slim chance, I know, but it might help us in our search."

"I've studied and studied this one myself," Judy said as she handed her a copy of that first poem Emily Grimshaw had given her as a test. No wonder she had said there was too much truth in it! The tower of flame, the ghosts— all, all of it might be true. Even the "human tomcat" that the poet had mentioned they believed to mean Irene's father, Tom Lang.

Now, through these very poems, Irene had found her mother's people. It would be such a thrilling, romantic thing to happen if only

they could talk it over with her. If only they
knew where she was. If only she hadn't taken
the manuscripts . . .

Judy showed Pauline the poem that Jasper
Crosby had brought in after Irene's disappearance. Now that they knew where Irene must
have been, they both saw new significance in
the lines:

Death cannot touch the halo of your hair.
Though, like a ghost, you disappear at will.
I knew you'd come in answer to my
prayer . . .
You, gentle sprite, whom love alone can
kill . . .

"Jasper Crosby never killed her with love,"
Pauline said bitterly. "I only hope——"

"Don't say it, Pauline!"

She looked sorry. "I won't say anything
more. We'll just keep on hoping."

Five o'clock came and Judy closed her desk
with a sigh.

"We've worked hard," she said to Pauline,
"but I just feel as if another day has been
wasted. While we sit here who knows what
may be happening to Irene?"

"At least we know that beastly uncle of hers can't be hurting her any more."

Judy thought of Pauline's statement in connection with death—not to be hurt any more. Old people wanted that kind of peace, that freedom from pain and fear. Death could be kind to old people who were through with romance and adventure. But Irene had so much to live for.

"The boys must be there ahead of us," Judy remarked as she and Pauline came in sight of the house. "See, someone has raised the window."

"They probably burnt something," Pauline said shortly.

Apparently she had misgivings concerning Peter's ability as a cook. It was early for them to be home. Why, it couldn't have been an hour since they left the police station in Parkville and there would be shopping for them to do besides.

As they turned down the corridor that led to Pauline's room Judy heard a familiar yowl. Could it be Blackberry asking to be let out?

"But he wasn't in," Pauline said. "Don't

you remember? We left him on the roof garden."

"Maybe the boys let him in. But it's queer they're not making any noise. You open the door, Pauline," Judy whispered. "I have the strangest feeling that something is about to happen."

Pauline hesitated, glanced at Judy and caught her hand as the door swung open. Neither of the girls had touched it!

# CHAPTER XXV

## THE HAPPY ENDING

PAULINE stood transfixed while Judy gathered Irene in her arms. If people fainted for joy she would have done it then. At first there were no explanations. Neither Judy nor Pauline expected any. The supreme realization that Irene was there—alive, safe—sufficed. Kisses were mingled with tears as Pauline, too, pressed closer to the golden-haired girl. If they had ever doubted Irene's sincerity, suspected her of anything, it was all forgotten at the moment.

"It's so good to see you again," Irene said at last. "There was nobody but Blackberry here to welcome me when I came in. It was almost as quiet as the house in Parkville after my grandmother died."

"Poor you!" Judy cried. "We found out all about that wicked uncle of yours and he's in jail now. Believe me, Irene, he wanted to get your grandmother's property and would have

done anything to be rid of you.  Oh, I'm so—
glad—you're safe——"

But Judy was sobbing again, clinging to
Irene as if she might vanish if she released her
hand.  Together she and Pauline led her to the
sofa where each of them found a seat close beside her.

It was growing dark and Judy lit the bridge
lamp.  It shone down on Irene's hair.  Something brighter than lamplight glowed, suddenly,
in her eyes.

"Where's Dale?" she asked.  "Has he
missed me?"

"He thinks of nothing but you," Judy answered.  "Horace and Peter and Arthur are
here, too.  All of them were hunting for you."

"How thrilling!  Did they like Dale, too?"

"Everybody likes him," Pauline put in.
"Lucky girl!  They say absence makes the
heart grow fonder, and I shouldn't wonder if
he fell in love with you."

"Really?"

"I'm almost sure of it," Pauline replied.
She spoke softly and only Irene heard her.
Judy ran to the window.

"They're coming!  I heard their voices.

Dale!" she called down to the street. "Arthur! Peter! Dale! Hurry!"

That was all she said. That was all she needed to say. The trembling joy in her voice told them the rest. In less time than seemed possible Dale burst through the half-open door.

"Irene!" he cried. "Am I dreaming or is this my lost princess, my Golden Girl?"

"What's he talking about?" Horace said gruffly to Judy. "Are they engaged?"

Judy smiled, watching their embrace. "Not yet, but we can guess they will be before long."

Dale and Irene faced the others. Radiance was in their faces.

"It's been quite a detective story," Dale said, "and this is the happy ending. Now, Irene, dear, suppose we go out on the roof garden—all of us—and you explain everything. I'm perfectly sure you can."

The others followed, eager to hear the story they had nearly given up hope of hearing from Irene's own lips. It proved to be almost identical with Jasper Crosby's story. Irene had not been forced to stay in her grandmother's house. She had stayed of her own free will because the old lady was sick and needed her.

"At first it was fun, almost like playing princess," Irene said. "I let her call me Joy and I called her Mother. I pretended to remember things my own mother must have done. I read aloud from her books and wore her dresses. This is one." She touched the simple white silk dress she was wearing and explained that she had intended to wear it to her grandmother's funeral. "But then Uncle Jasper decided that I must not go. He said that being with her when she died had affected my mind. I believed him then but now that I'm home again I feel sure that it wasn't true. Still, there's something like a magnet that just draws me back to that dear old house."

"Your grandmother's house?"

"My house now, isn't it, Peter?"

The young law student looked up with a start. He had forgotten all about the will in the excitement of having Irene safe again. But she had changed so! He couldn't quite understand this new, beautiful Irene—this Irene who was an heiress.

"Why, er—yes," he said. "I believe everything is legally yours, even the royalties from that new book Emily Grimshaw is publishing."

Dale and Judy looked first at each other and then at Irene. Both of them were wondering the same thing. How could Emily Grimshaw have the book published if the manuscripts were missing? Dale was the first to put the thought into words.

"They aren't missing any more," Irene replied and darted back inside the door. When the others had joined her in Pauline's sitting room she opened a small suitcase that stood on the floor and gave the papers a toss onto the table.

"There they are—every blessed one of them. I packed them with my things so Uncle Jasper wouldn't see me take them. Why don't you give them all back to Emily Grimshaw in the morning?"

"But what will I tell her?" gasped Judy. "I can't tell her you stole them. What will I say? Oh, why did you do it? Can't you see all the trouble it has caused? Really, Irene, you're dreadfully hard-hearted."

"Am I?" The golden-haired girl smiled wanly. "And all the time I thought you were, not to come and see me."

"How could we have come?"

"I told you in my letter. It explained everything but now, oh, now it's going to be harder to explain."

"What letter? Did you get a letter?" Dale turned and demanded of Judy.

"Of course I didn't."

"Then how did you find out where I was?"

Peter explained this question to Irene. He told her about the radio broadcast, the police activities and how earnestly all of them had searched. It seemed that the tables had turned and they, not Irene, were doing the explaining. But what could have happened to Irene's letter? She said she had written three.

"I gave them to Uncle Jasper to mail——"

Judy interrupted with a little cry. "There's your explanation. He must have destroyed them. The miserable old cheat! Was he mean to you, Irene?"

She sighed. "This is the part I hardly dare tell. He made me think it was an—an hallucination. You know, like crazy people get. But I was in the tower lying on my bed. I'd been up all night and he told me to rest. It was right after Grandma died. Well, he moved the bed across the room—way across and I

felt a little queer as if it weren't quite safe. I
knew the tower was only propped up. Then he
got ugly. He told me I was going insane. He
said if I didn't lie in the bed he'd tie me there.
So I lay down. In a little while I heard some
one rapping on the door and I ran to the window. I saw you, Judy, but you didn't hear me
call. You were almost out of sight. Then I
looked down, and, as sure as I'm alive, there
was Uncle Jasper taking the props out from
under the tower. One of them fell and struck
him across the chest. I think,'' she added,
turning to Peter, ''that there must be marks on
his chest to prove that what I say is true.''

''It's a serious charge, Irene. He could do
twenty years for that. But he deserves it if
what you say is true.''

''It's true. And, oh, I was so frightened. I
ran downstairs and I guess I was screaming—
or crying—or both. Anyway, he quit hammer-
ing at the props. He had a sledge hammer and
a long beam to work with. That was so the
tower wouldn't fall on him.''

''You remember that long beam we used to
break down the door?'' Dale interrupted her
to ask.

Both Judy and Peter nodded. Their faces were grave. Blackberry, who possessed a cat's inborn capacity for sympathy, came forth from his corner and looked up at Irene. She patted him as she went on talking.

"Uncle Jasper got scared then. He said he'd have to get me back to my father in a hurry. He explained how he was really putting more props under the tower and said it was because my mind wasn't right that I had been afraid he would kill me. He told me that if I didn't want to go to the insane asylum I'd keep still about the whole thing. I said I would but it wasn't true and I'm sure he didn't believe me. Then he took me riding in the car but he didn't take the road for Farringdon. I don't know where he intended to take me but wherever it was, I didn't want to go. So, when he had to slow down for a railroad crossing, I jumped out of the car. He was busy driving and didn't miss me until afterwards. By that time I had started hiking. So here I am and I guess that explains everything."

Irene sank back in her chair and looked, suddenly, tired. Judy realized that she must be hungry too. She remembered the packages that

the boys had brought in, and all of them set
about preparing food and something for Irene
to drink. She wanted coffee with plenty of
cream. The same Irene, dear child! Judy
didn't care if she never explained about the
poetry.

# CHAPTER XXVI

THE meal that Peter Dobbs cooked and served was a merry one. Truly, it was an occasion for rejoicing.

"A party after all," Dale said. He told Irene about the other party and how they waited and waited.

Judy sat between Arthur and Peter dividing her attention between them. She rose, lifted her glass of water and gave a toast:

"Happiness for all of us! Here's how!"

Her gayety was contagious. Everybody was laughing now. It was good to be able to laugh with Irene again. She was just meant to be spoiled and laughed with Dale declared.

Horace brought in dessert. Like children at a birthday party everybody screamed, "Ice cream! Hurray for ice cream!"

"And cake," he added. "It's a little late, Irene, but we might call this your birthday cake."

He placed a foamy creation of walnuts and chocolate at her place. She cut the first slice for Dale and the second slice for Horace.

"Now you, Judy," she went on, flourishing the knife, "and a little crumb for Blackberry."

The cat caught it in his paws and played with it, like a mouse, before he ate it.

"To think that I used to dislike him," Dale said apologetically.

Everyone was served now. Judy remembered the two extra candles left over from the party that hadn't been a party. She brought them out and Irene lit them. How golden everything looked in their light! Irene's eyes shone. Her hair was a halo around her head.

"You're beautiful," Dale said softly.

Judy heard him and smiled, sharing their happiness. She turned to the others. "It's worth waiting for—this kind of a party, isn't it, people?"

"We'll dance afterwards," Pauline suggested. She excused herself to turn on the radio, hoping to tune in on Irene's song. But before she found anything worth while the doorbell rang.

"I'll answer it," Irene cried. "I feel like

surprising somebody and I'm sure, whoever it is, they'll be terribly surprised.''

They were all watching Irene as she danced toward the door, quite unprepared for the kind of surprise that awaited her on the other side.

She swung it open.  There, framed in the doorway, stood Her Majesty, Emily Grimshaw.

"I've come to settle with you, Joy Holiday," she shouted and raised a threatening finger at Irene.

The three boys stared in blank bewilderment. They had never seen this strange old lady and imagined that she must be an escaped inmate from some near-by asylum—except that she had used the now familiar name, Joy Holiday.

Chairs were pushed back from the table. Dale Meredith rose and strode over to the door, followed by Judy and Peter.

"What's this?" the indignant young author demanded.  "Miss Grimshaw, what's the big idea of storming in here and frightening Irene?"

"Who has a better right?" she retorted belligerently.

Taking her gently by the shoulders, Peter pushed her into a chair.  "Sit down quietly now while we finish dinner. No need to raise a row about it. I'm sure Irene will be glad to listen to what you have to say."

"Irene, nothing!" she fumed. "That girl's Johanna Holiday, the wench who made away with her mother's poetry. I know you!" She pointed a shaking finger at the trembling Irene.

Judy, standing near the old lady, caught a whiff of her breath and guessed that she had taken an overdose from the bottle that she called her tonic. She had noticed how frequently her employer resorted to the stimulant. After a few drinks she always talked freely of spirits. But Judy was in no mood for listening to ghost stories now.

"I know you!" the indomitable old lady repeated. "I saw you, Joy Holiday, just before your mother's funeral. Break her heart while she lived and then come back to gloat over her when she's dead. You're a devil, you are. Only devils are immune to death."

Dale moved closer to Irene as if to ward off the blows that must come to her senses with the old lady's words.

"We've got to get her out of here," Peter whispered hoarsely to Dale.

"No! No!" Judy protested. "We must be civil to her. There's some black coffee on the stove. That may sober her up a bit, and after all we did want to see her."

"Then let's get Irene out of the room."

"You take her out on the roof garden, Dale," Judy begged. "I'm used to being alone with Miss Grimshaw."

He protested at first but when he saw that the black coffee was doing its work he finally slipped quietly out of the door, an arm about Irene's waist.

"What's the trouble?" Horace whispered. He and Arthur couldn't understand Emily Grimshaw's grievance.

"Too much excitement," Judy stated briefly. "She was at the poet's funeral and thinks Irene is her mother's ghost. We'll be able to reason with her after a bit."

"But what does she mean about the poetry?" Horace insisted.

Judy, however, would say nothing more. She turned her attention to the old lady now, endeavoring to engage her in a sensible conversation. "So you were at the funeral, Miss Grimshaw. I wondered why you hadn't come in to the office. When did Sarah Glenn die?"

"Lord knows!" Emily Grimshaw answered. "But I went out there to pay my respects to the dead. Heard about it through friends. And there was that—that—that——"

Her voice trailed off in a groan. She was pointing again but this time not at Irene but at the vacant spot where the girl had stood.

"Good Lord! She's gone again."

"She went out quietly," Judy explained. "Dale Meredith was with her. They'll be back."

"They'd better be," the irate woman answered. "Those poems had better be back too or I'll know the reason why. Ghost or no ghost, that girl can't get away with stealing——"

"Your poems are here," Judy interrupted, her voice quiet but firm. She lifted the stack of papers from the desk, and before Emily Grimshaw could get her breath, she had deposited them in the startled old lady's lap. "Now," she continued, "after you finish another cup of this nice strong coffee, I'll call Dale and the girl back into the room and all of us can hear her story."

"You mean Joy Holiday?"

"I mean the girl you call Joy Holiday. The real Joy Holiday is dead. You see, she didn't vanish as you thought she did. She climbed down from the tower window and eloped with her lover. This girl is her daughter and she was wearing her mother's yellow dress the day you saw her."

Emily Grimshaw sat forward in her chair and passed her hand across her eyes.

"Say that again. It didn't—register."

Judy laughed. She could see that her employer was coming back to her senses.

"You tell her, Horace." She motioned to her brother who had been sitting beside the table with Pauline and Arthur, listening.

Joy Holiday's story was a real romance, however badly told. But Horace Bolton, the reporter, made the tale so vivid that the five who heard it lived the adventure all over again. Whatever else it did, it cleared Emily Grimshaw's clouded brain and brought the old, practical look back into her eyes.

Arthur wound up by telling of his search by air for Irene's distracted father. Now, if only Irene could explain about the poetry, they had nothing to fear.

Opening the door quietly, Judy beckoned to
the two figures who sat in the hammock.  As
Dale stood up, outlined against the sky, it reminded her of that first night that she and
Pauline had found them there and they had
been invited to that never-to-be-forgotten dance
on the hotel roof garden.  She caught Irene's
hand as she entered the door.  Impulsively she
kissed her.

"Tell us about it now, dear," she murmured.
"The boys and I will understand and I'm sure
Pauline will too.  And if Emily Grimshaw gets
another queer spell we'll send her packing with
her precious poetry.  We have what we want
—you."

The agent looked up as Irene entered the
room.  She stared for a moment as if the girl's
golden beauty fascinated her.  Then she passed
one hand across her forehead, smoothing out
the furrows that twenty years had left there.
The light of understanding came into her eyes.

"You are . . . you are the image of your
mother," she said at last.  "While you live
Joy Holiday will never be dead."

" 'Death cannot touch the halo of your

hair,' " Judy quoted dreamily. "After all, it
is a beautiful thought, Irene. There's nothing
uncanny about that kind of a spirit."

"Don't talk spirits to her," the agent
snapped.

Her seriousness brought to Judy's mind the
phantom shape she had seen in the tower window. Disregarding her, she asked Irene to tell
her about it.

The girl laughed, that familiar silvery laugh.

"It frightened me too," she admitted, "until Uncle Jasper told me it was only a reflection.
Then it seemed stupid of me not to have
guessed it. He said any sane person would
have. But you're sane, Judy, and you didn't."

"That proves there's no truth in what he
said," Horace assured her.

It was a great satisfaction to Irene, knowing
that. She sighed and went on explaining about
the ghost in the tower.

"You know, the room is round and there are
windows on all sides. Between the windows are
mirrors that make the oddest reflections. I
must have been standing in the room so that
you could see the mirror but not me. I should

think you would have been scared to death.''

''And then you pulled the shades?'' Judy anticipated.

''No, I didn't. Uncle Jasper did, just before he went down and started taking the props out from under the tower. That must have been after you left.''

''We saw the mirrors afterwards, too—and your yellow dress. But that was when we searched the house. You were gone by then.''

''Yes, and Grandma was gone, too. Poor soul! It really made me happy to think she could die in peace, believing that her golden girl still lived. That poem you just quoted, Judy, was written to me. She thought I was immune to death.''

''Well, people never do die if you look at it that way,'' Judy said thoughtfully. ''Your mother's beauty was reborn in you, and you may pass it on to your children and their children——''

''What about your children?'' Arthur asked, smiling quizzically at Judy.

''Oh, me? I'm too young to be thinking about them. My career comes first. Now I'm sure

Chief Kelly will listen to me when I tell him I want to be a detective.''

They all agreed. No one could doubt that solving mysteries was Judy's one great talent.

And yet—the missing poetry was still unexplained.

# CHAPTER XXVII

ALL this time Emily Grimshaw had not taken her eyes away from Irene. Now she turned to the others, contrition written in every line of her face.

"I see it all now," she murmured. "And I've been as big a fool as Sarah Glenn for all she was supposed to be crazy."

"Perhaps it was the fault of that tonic you've been taking," Peter suggested, his eyes twinkling wickedly.

"Piffle!" the old lady snorted. "That's good stuff, bottled in bond. A wee bit strong, though," she added, shaking her head, "a wee —bit—strong."

Emily Grimshaw had her poetry and rose, a little unsteadily, preparing to leave. It was then that she thought of the purpose of her visit.

"Young woman," she demanded of Irene, "if

198

you're not Joy Holiday, why did you take those manuscripts?''

"I didn't take them," the accused girl answered, regarding her steadily with those starry eyes that had inspired the loveliest line of *Golden Girl*.

Judy made an almost inaudible sound of protest. Irene couldn't keep on denying it. No one would believe her now. She touched her arm and whispered, "Tell her, dear. It's no good pretending. The rest of us have forgiven you and I'm sure she will too."

Irene's eyes widened. "Forgiven me? For what, may I ask? Why, I didn't see that poetry from the moment it was taken until I found it lying on my grandmother's table."

"You expect us to believe that, Irene?" This was Peter's voice, the voice he would some day use in the court room.

Dale turned on him. "Of course she does. And I do believe it. Sarah Glenn may have taken her own poetry——"

"When she was too sick to move out of her house?"

"Or Jasper Crosby may have sneaked into the office," Dale went on, disregarding his ques-

tion. "Irene says she didn't take the poems
and that ends the matter once and forever. If
the rest of you want to go on distrusting her
it's none of my affair but I knew all along that
Irene was too fine, too wonderful——"

Irene herself stopped him. Her voice was
almost a command. "Leave them alone, Dale.
Why shouldn't they suspect me?"

"Because you didn't do it."

Irene was silent. She couldn't say any more
because the last she knew of the poems they
were in Judy's hands. It was after all lights
were out and they were in bed that she told her.

"You said never to mind the work; you'd
straighten things. And then some one took
the poetry out of my hands. Wasn't it you?"

"It certainly wasn't," Judy declared. "I
had just opened the door for Dale Meredith but
he wasn't there yet."

"Did you turn your back? Could anyone
else have come in?"

"Why," Judy exclaimed, "I believe they
could have—if they had been very quick."

"Uncle Jasper is quick. But why would he
take the poetry?"

Now Judy knew! It was like a heavy load

falling from her shoulders. She remembered what Emily Grimshaw had said about his suing her. He had schemed to do it and stolen the poetry himself. Besides, he may have suspected Irene's identity and been afraid she would find out too much.

Irene's eyes sought Judy's and found in them understanding and sympathy. She had told the truth, and, with Judy to explain, everyone would believe her. But she couldn't forget that it was Dale Meredith who had believed her without an explanation.

# CHAPTER XXVIII

Two weeks later Dale Meredith came into Emily Grimshaw's office and under his arm he carried a new book manuscript. It was the day that Pauline took over Judy's position—with her father's consent. Dr. Faulkner was home now, as busy and professional as ever. But he had not been too busy to listen to the smallest detail of Irene's remarkable story. She wanted his advice as a brain specialist. Was it fair with insanity in the family——

Dr. Faulkner had not let her finish the sentence. Of course it was fair. Sarah Glenn had once been a patient of his and he declared that she was only slightly eccentric—not insane until her brother had driven her to it.

"And don't you know that this type of insanity cannot be inherited?" he had asked Irene. "There's no need to worry your pretty head about that. Under the same conditions,

202

perhaps. But those conditions cannot exist with Jasper Crosby in prison. And do quit calling him Uncle Jasper. He's no blood relation, only a stepbrother, and Glenn was really your grandmother's maiden name.''

"Oh, Father, if you had only been home before!" Pauline had exclaimed.

The doctor had smiled that rare smile of his. "Dr. Bolton's daughter did wonders without me," he had said.

Then Pauline knew that her father would not object to Judy's plans for her. He hadn't wanted her to work before. Now it pleased him to know she was filling Judy's position.

"You've been working hard, Dale," Pauline said, glancing up from the manuscript he had just given her. She was seated at her new desk, looking very professional.

Judy stood beside the table straightening out a few of her things as she wanted to leave the office in perfect order.

But Dale Meredith expected these girls to show more than a professional interest in his story. He had put his heart into it—and his experience.

Judy smiled. "Is it another detective story?"

"It's the greatest detective story you'll ever read. The detective is a sixteen-year-old girl."

"Sounds interesting. What does she look like?"

For answer Dale walked over to the little mirror where Judy usually stood to arrange her hat. He took it down from the wall and held it so that Judy's bright hair and clear gray eyes were reflected in its surface.

"There! That's my detective. Irene is the heroine. She has the original manuscript reading it now. Our whole future depends on what she thinks of the ending."

"Really, Dale? Is it as serious as that?"

"It was serious enough for me to invest in this. Do you think she'll like it?"

He took from his pocket a tiny square box. Opening it, he displayed a ring that would, had Judy known it, play an important part in another mystery that she was to solve. It was a beautiful thing. Beautiful chiefly because it was so simple, just a solitaire set in a gold band and decorated with almost invisible orange blossoms.

"I even had it engraved," he said and then blushed, a thing Judy had never known Dale Meredith to do before.

"I don't know why I'm showing it to you girls," he said. "Perhaps I shouldn't. She might rather show it herself."

Snapping shut the lid, he put it hastily back in his pocket. He stood as if waiting for something.

"I'll be almost afraid to read your story if it's all true, Dale," Judy said. "It will be so much like—like—" She floundered for a word.

"Like spying on me?"

"Something like that."

"Well, it isn't all true—only the important part. You'll both read it, won't you?"

"Of course we'll read it. That's what we're being paid for, isn't it, Pauline?"

The book was a revelation. Dale had made a murder mystery out of the very thing that had happened to Irene. Jasper Crosby's scheme to wreck the tower had worked in the story, killing the grandmother instead of Irene. The names were different. But for that Judy saw herself moving through the pages of his story, playing the part of the clever girl detective. She saw Pauline's faults depicted. All the petty jealousies she had felt were revealed, used to cast suspicion upon her and then excused, baring the real girl underneath. The Golden Girl of Dale's story was Irene in her mother's dress. Dale, himself, was the narrator and the suspense, the worry and, finally, the romance of the story were things he had felt and written with feeling. Judy found a new and lovelier Irene in Dale's description of her. She marveled that he understood every one of them so well. The boys came, appropriately, at the end and, through it all, the spark of humor was the literary agent.

When Emily Grimshaw came in neither Judy nor Pauline looked up. They did not hear her enter the room. Finally she stood over them and spoke in a sharp tone.

"What's this you're reading? Didn't I tell you to get done with your typewriting first? Letters are important but manuscripts can always wait to be read."

"This one can't," Judy replied, smiling up at her employer. "This is Dale Meredith's new detective story. Irene is the heroine, Pauline one of the suspects and I am the detective."

"So! And I suppose I am the criminal."

Judy startled the old lady by kissing her.

"You are your own sweet self, Miss Grimshaw. It will surprise you what a lovable person you are. Why don't you read the book and get acquainted?"

Turning pages broke the silence in the office all that day. Clients that came in were hastily dismissed. Other work waited. Dale Meredith had written life itself in the pages of a book that would make him famous.

He called for the girls at five o'clock.

"What did you think of it?" He asked when they failed to mention his work.

"Wonderful!" Pauline breathed.

"And you, Judy?"

"I'm still filled with it," she replied, "too much to talk. Anyway, I'm going home and there won't be time to talk. Irene is going also."

"Why on earth?"

"Because Peter has promised to take her in his car."

"He's been taking her out a good deal lately," Dale said, his brow darkening.

"Why shouldn't he?" Pauline asked. "Peter

is a nice boy and Irene needs somebody to help her plan things.''

"She knows I'd be glad to help her."

"I'm sure she does. But she needs Peter's legal advice," Judy explained. "He says the chief thing they talk about is what to do with Sarah Glenn's house. Irene says she wants to live in it."

"Alone?" Pauline asked.

"No, with her father. He's still depending on her and she is so glad to be able to take care of him the way she's always wanted to. His room is to be that big sunny one in the front of the house. There's room for Irene's piano in it and he loves to hear her play. But the tower room she wants kept just the way her mother had it. Oh, she's talked of it so much —even to selecting the kind of flowers she wants in the garden."

"She told me," Dale said, but his simple remark set Judy wondering how much they had told each other. It seemed strange for little Irene to be having a real romance. She was so young! Too young, Judy would have thought if she had not realized how much Irene needed the love and sense of security that a man like Dale Meredith could give her.

Bright-eyed and smiling, Irene looked the part of a heroine when she met them at the door. Dale promptly took possession of her and, for an hour, nothing more was heard from either of them except a low murmur of voices on the roof garden.

In the meantime Arthur had arrived dressed in his flying gear and ready to take Judy home. She and her cat were both to fly with him in his open plane.

It was decided that Irene would ride with Horace in Peter's car and stay with the Dobbs family while she was in Farringdon. That would give her time to collect her few things and, as soon as her father was able to travel, they would both come back to live in Tower House

"We named it that," Irene said. "Dale and I."

"It sounds romantic," Judy answered. "May I come and visit?"

"You certainly may. And you must come for the celebration."

"You mean the housewarming as soon as you and your father have Tower House fixed up?"

Irene's eyes danced. "Oh, no! Dale's supervising that. I mean celebrating the success of his new book. I read it today. And it will be a success," she said softly. "Thanks to you, Judy, it's all true, even the happy ending."

**THE END**

# The Judy Bolton Mystery Stories
## By *MARGARET SUTTON*

Judy's adventures, every one of them, have been based on something that actually happened. The flood, the house with the round attic windows, the hiding place of the invisible chimes, the school fire, the camp in the Thousand Islands, the queer old house in Parkville and the panic in the theatre —all of them are real!

*You will not want to miss one of these thrilling stories.*

THE VANISHING SHADOW—Judy is constantly pursued by a mysterious shadow. Her brother, a timid but lovable boy, turns out to be a real hero in this dramatic, fast moving story.

THE HAUNTED ATTIC—The Boltons move into a large rambling house reputed to be haunted. Even brave Judy is frightened at the strange rappings and the eerie "crying ghost".

THE INVISIBLE CHIMES—A strange girl is sheltered by the Boltons and Judy tracks down many clues before she uncovers her real identity.

SEVEN STRANGE CLUES—Judy works out seven baffling clues to solve the mystery of a school fire and a prize poster contest.

THE GHOST PARADE—Weird happenings at Thousand Island Camp provide mystery, humor and adventure in this thrilling story.

THE YELLOW PHANTOM—With her quick thinking and courage, Judy rescues a lost friend and solves the mystery of "Golden Girl."

THE MYSTIC BALL—Irene, "the engaged girl," is frightened by a crystal gazer but Judy exposes the trickery and saves her friend's romance.

THE VOICE IN THE SUITCASE—A weird cry leads Judy into excitement and danger in a lonely old house.

THE MYSTERIOUS HALF CAT—Judy and her friends become suspicious of a mysterious old beggar and follow him.

GROSSET & DUNLAP     *Publishers*     NEW YORK

# DANA GIRLS MYSTERY STORIES

## By CAROLYN KEENE

*Author of the*
NANCY DREW MYSTERY STORIES

Impetuous, delightful Jean Dana and her charming serious minded sister Louise find themselves in the midst of several mysteries, when they attempt to aid people who are in trouble. Thrilling moments come to the girls as they follow up clue after clue in an endeavor to untangle the knotty problems in which they become enmeshed.

### BY THE LIGHT OF THE STUDY LAMP

A stolen study lamp, a fortune teller, and a distressed schoolmate provide plenty of excitement for the Dana girls before they locate the persons responsible for many mysterious happenings.

### THE SECRET AT LONE TREE COTTAGE

While the girls are at Starhurst School, they learn that their beloved English teacher has vanished in a strange manner. In tracing her, Jean and Louise are able to aid the frantic relatives of a dear little curly-haired tot, but not before they themselves are in danger of disappearing.

### IN THE SHADOW OF THE TOWER

The mingling of unusual characters, who have life interests very different from one another, lends excitement and intrigue to a Christmas vacation of the Dana girls. Their ability to fit together the pieces of a strange puzzle brings happiness to several persons.

### A THREE-CORNERED MYSTERY

There were three strange corners which the Dana girls successfully rounded in their search for clues to clear up a mystery, involving property and an international spy of many aliases.

### THE SECRET AT THE HERMITAGE

When Louise is mistaken for a runaway prisoner, strange things begin to happen, which lead the Danas to uncover the secret of a talented girl and her crippled charge.

GROSSET & DUNLAP : *Publishers* : NEW YORK

*There is the high, happy spirit of youth in these famous*

# BOOKS FOR GIRLS
## by JANE D. ABBOTT

### BARBERRY GATE
A boy flyer opened the Barberry Gate, closed since the day great-grandfather Colfax locked it, and Winsome learned the romantic story behind it all.

### LAUGHING LAST
Sidney finds adventure in Provincetown—she takes part in the capture of modern pirates, and much to her surprise plays an unexpected part in her sister's romance.

### APRILLY
The charming story of a young girl, child of the circus, and the adventures which led to her goal of happiness.

### HIGHACRES
A school story of Jerry Travis and her chum Gyp Westley. A thread of romance and mystery in Jerry's life runs through the tale.

### KEINETH
How Keineth Randolph kept a secret—a war secret—for a whole year makes one of the best stories ever written for girls.

### RED ROBIN
In attempting to bring happiness into the lives of mill workers, Robin Forsythe, heir to a fortune, has many strange adventures.

### HEYDAY
Twenty-three! The heyday of life. Jay, a small town girl, finds happiness in New York.

### LARKSPUR
Especially interesting to any Girl Scout because it is the story of a Girl Scout who is poor and has to help her mother.

### HAPPY HOUSE
How an old family quarrel is healed through a misunderstanding and an old homestead becomes a "happy house" in reality.

GROSSET & DUNLAP     *Publishers*     NEW YORK

# Melody Lane Mystery Stories

## By LILIAN GARIS

Thrills, secrets, ghosts—adventures that will fascinate you seem to surround pretty Carol Duncan. A vivid, plucky girl, her cleverness at solving mysteries will captivate and thrill every mystery fan.

The author has written many popular mystery stories for girls and in this new series Mrs. Garis is at her best.

### THE GHOST OF MELODY LANE

Mystery surrounds the great organ in the home of the "Cameo Lady"—beloved friend of Carol and sponsor of the girls' Coral Club. Three people see the "ghost" that wanders in the grove carrying a waxy white rose. And Carol finds the rose! In the end she finds the ghost too!

### THE FORBIDDEN TRAIL

There was a tradition at "Splatter Castle" on Melody Lane, and Marah Splartier, eccentric aunt of Veronica Flint determined to protect Vera from following the long line of family tragedies that had had their beginning on the "forbidden trail." Carol has several bad frights before she clears up the mystery that keeps the little family at Splatter Castle unhappy and afraid.

### THE TOWER SECRET

The winking lights flashing from the old tower on the grounds of the Bonds' new home defy explanation. There is no one in the tower—and no electric power or connections! Had the engaging circus family that Carol befriended anything to do with the mystery? And what interest had Parsnips, the queer old farmer, in the "ghost" tower?

### THE WILD WARNING

What power did the strange, wild warning in the woods have over Polly Flinders? And why was she so desperately anxious to earn money? Carol brings happiness to three families when she solves this exciting mystery.

### THE TERROR OF MOANING CLIFF

No tenant would stay in the great, bleak house on "moaning cliff" that belonged to Carol's aunt. But Carol, courageous and determined, finally tracks the uncanny "haunts" to their source.

### THE DRAGON OF THE HILLS

When Carol runs a tea shop for a friend, a baffling mystery comes to her with her first customer. Who has the limping man's lost package—the gypsies, the oriental or the neighbor's boy who ran away?

GROSSET & DUNLAP          *Publishers*          NEW YORK